ATALANTA
AND THE
ARCADIAN
BEAST

YOUNG HEROES

ATALANTA
AND THE
ARCADIAN
BEAST

By
JANE YOLEN
and
ROBERT J. HARRIS

■■ HarperCollins*Publishers*

J
YOL

Library of Congress Cataloging-in-Publication Data
Yolen, Jane.
    Atalanta and the Arcadian Beast / by Jane Yolen and Robert J. Harris.
    p.   cm. — (Young heroes)
    Summary: Twelve-year-old Atalanta seeks revenge on the mysterious creature that killed her
adoptive father, and with the help of her bear friend Urso, hunts down the beast, meets the
legendary hunter Orion, and discovers the truth of her parentage.
    ISBN 0-06-029454-X — ISBN 0-06-029455-8 (lib. bdg.)
    1. Atalanta (Greek mythology)—Juvenile fiction. [1. Atalanta (Greek mythology)—Fiction.
2. Orion (Greek mythology)—Fiction. 3. Mythology, Greek—Fiction. 4. Adventure and
adventurers—Fiction. 5. Heroes—Fiction.] I. Harris, Robert J., 1955– II. Title. III. Series.
PZ7.Y78 At 2003   2001051746
[Fic]—dc21   CIP
                                                                                              AC

Typography by Carla Weise
1 2 3 4 5 6 7 8 9 10
❖
First Edition

1\04- B+T- 15.99

For Heidi—
who keeps me running
on the right path
—J.Y.

To David E. Poole and
Professor Robert Ogilvie, who taught me
Homer and Virgil and much else besides
—R.J.H.

Contents

CHAPTER ONE

A SHAPE IN THE FOREST

The girl was silent, tracking through the deep woods, a small gutted rabbit safely tucked into her leather belt. It was all she had found in the snares they'd set, and she was still hoping she might be able to find something more impressive before her father reappeared.

He'd left her to check the snares while he followed some deer tracks. Of course she'd grumbled. Checking the traps was a child's task.

"And I'm no longer a child," she whispered to herself, though she wasn't yet thirteen.

The forest seemed unnaturally quiet. Nothing scrabbled in the underbrush away from her. No birds trilled overhead. Even the wood pigeons were still. She was disappointed.

How can I prove to Papa what a good hunter I am, she thought, *if there is nothing here to hunt?*

A spring gurgled from a low crag, their usual meeting place. Glancing around, she looked for some sign of her father.

Perhaps he has had good luck, she thought. Then she added in an under-breath, "I've certainly had none." The rabbit didn't count. It was scarcely a meal for one, and besides, it had been caught in their snares.

Setting aside her bow, she crouched by the stream and scooped up the cool water in her cupped hands, drinking greedily. Then she straightened up, licking the droplets from her lips and brushing a strand of dark hair from her eyes in a single unconsciously graceful movement.

The sun was almost touching the hilltops to the west.

Where is he? she wondered, a bit anxious. They had agreed to meet long before dark. It was not like him to be late.

The only other time he'd left her waiting at the stream was a few weeks ago when he'd been gathering wildflowers for her birth remembrance day. She'd forgotten about it. He hadn't.

She smiled at the memory, then stiffened at a sudden noise, a strange rustling in the bushes, as if something big was creeping through the undergrowth toward her.

It didn't sound like her father.

Instantly alert, she snatched up her bow and looked about.

As suddenly as it had come, the noise was gone.

A breeze? she thought. *A breeze could rustle the bushes.* But she didn't really believe it was a breeze. Or at least she wasn't sure of it. In the woods—her father always said—certainty keeps the hunter alive.

She slipped an arrow out of her quiver and fitted it to the bowstring.

The rustling started again, and this time there was no breeze. Then she heard a solid *crack,* as if a branch had been stepped upon.

A deer? Too heavy.

A boar? Too subtle.

A bear? Though they were rare in these parts.

A pair of wood pigeons burst suddenly from a tree, their wings beating in a desperate flight. The girl felt her heart fly off with them.

Suddenly something touched her on her arm and she whirled about, arrow at the ready.

"Papa!" She lowered the bow.

"Hush, Atalanta," he said, raising a finger to his lips. "There's something out there." His weather-browned face creased with concern. "Something big."

"I know," she whispered back, realizing she *did* know. "I think it may be stalking me. What is it?"

His eyes narrowed, and his fingers clenched tightly

around the shaft of his long hunting spear. "I don't know. I found some spoor in the woods. Nothing I recognize."

She thought, *Nothing* he *recognizes? How can that be?* Her father knew every inch of the forest. He was a great hunter. Perhaps the greatest. She found herself shivering.

"Nothing from around here, anyway," he added.

There was a small flicker of movement in the bushes, barely visible in the twilight. Atalanta caught a glimpse of a large tawny shape, low to the ground. Then in a blink of an eye it was gone again.

"Put away your bow," her father whispered, "and be ready to run."

"But I'm a hunter, too—" Atalanta began.

"Don't argue with me, Atalanta," he said, his voice low. "I *know* you are a hunter. But if we don't get away now, we'll be two *dead* hunters."

She had never heard him nervous like this. Nodding, she slipped the arrow carefully back into the quiver and slung the bow over her shoulder. She grasped the hilt of her knife where it was kept in her belt but did not draw it.

Her father hefted the spear above his head, drawing back his right arm. "Go!" he barked, his voice like the snap of a bowstring.

She shot into the copse of trees behind her, as fast as a rabbit fleeing a fox. Only once did she glance back, in time to see him hurl his spear at some shape that was ripping through the greenery toward him.

For a moment she hesitated, then heard him pounding behind her.

"Don't look back!" he called. "It will only slow you down." Then he caught up to her, his fingers digging into her shoulder, pushing her onward. "Run, Atalanta, run!"

From behind them came an incredible roar. It sounded like a cataract of rocks and boulders crashing down the slopes of Mount Parthenon.

All the hairs on the nape of Atalanta's neck seemed to stand up at the sound. She had always been quick, quick enough to match her father step for step when he sprinted through the forest after deer or wild goat. But that roar pushed her forward at a pace she'd never managed before.

This time they were not the hunters. They were the prey.

"Will we be fast enough?" she cried.

"Save your breath for running."

She ran.

As she ran, she thought: *We might have one advantage. Papa said the beast was not from around here.* She and her father had been hunting the woods for years. They knew every track and stream and shortcut and obstacle.

"Left, Papa!" she cried, taking a quick jog left and sliding through a small cleft in a wall of stone. Her father followed.

There! she thought, pleased when the beast behind

them roared its frustration.

But it must have found another way to scramble over the stone, for almost immediately it was on their trail again.

A thick copse of trees seemed to stymie it only momentarily.

They leaped a small stream but heard it close behind.

Atalanta could feel her breath searing her throat. "Papa," she gasped, but couldn't get out anything more.

"The house," he cried, his voice full of pain. "Safe there."

And there, across the clearing, was their cottage.

Atalanta took another hot breath and, with a final burst of speed, headed toward it. She could hear the thump of huge paws behind her, then remembered her father's warning not to look behind.

She was tiring, but a small prod in her back gave her the energy for a few more steps. Then a few more.

Suddenly, she could hear her father stop running; hear the sound of his knife slicing through the air; hear a grunt, a gasp, a cry.

Then she was at the cottage door, yanking it open, tumbling through, rolling across the straw-covered floor.

Her father was several steps behind her, and he came in through the door, gasping.

"Papa!" she cried, relieved he was all right.

He slammed the door shut, and she got up to help

him bar it, shoving the heavy wooden beam across.

No sooner was the beam in place than a huge weight crashed into the door, making the whole house shudder. Thankfully, the door held.

Her father slid to the floor with a groan. There was a bead of blood on his tunic.

No, Atalanta thought, *not a bead, a spot.* Then she thought: *Not a spot, a blot.* Even as she watched, the bloodstain grew bigger.

She knelt beside him, lifted the tunic, saw the wound. It was jagged and wide and blood seemed to be gurgling out like the spring from the crag.

"Papa!" she whispered.

He tried to answer but could only manage a croak. He pulled down the tunic and pressed his hand against it to try and staunch the bleeding.

From outside came a low growl followed by a snuffling noise. Something was sniffing at the door.

To her horror, Atalanta realized that the beast must be smelling the blood.

She pulled her father away from the door and got him up onto his pallet.

"Stay there, Papa," she said, but he did not hear her, having fainted with the pain.

Drawing her knife, she went back to the door where she stood silently for a moment, listening. The scratching and the growling came again, then stopped.

Her father had always said a hunter's ears were

among his most important weapons. She strained to understand what she was hearing. The beast seemed to be padding around the little house, rubbing itself against the rough stone walls as if marking its territory. Then it went around a second time.

The house had two small windows, each protected by a leather curtain. Those curtains were open. Atalanta stared out as the beast went by, its bulk blocking the light.

It's huge! she thought. *Big as a bear. Bigger.*

She kept listening as the thing made yet another circuit of the house. Her palm was clammy against the handle of the knife. Beads of sweat dripped down her face, tracing little rivulets.

Silently, she stepped over to one of the windows, pressed her back against the wall, and waited for the beast to pass by again.

It must have smelled her sweat or heard her breathing, for—like lightning—it stuck its huge paw through the window, sharp claws shredding the leather curtain.

Atalanta reacted without thinking, jamming the knife into the paw, right where a wrist would have been.

The beast roared with pain and jerked the paw back, knife and all. Then it roared again. This time the sound seemed compounded of rage and pain.

Standing frozen by the window, Atalanta found she could not move.

A groan from her father was so loud, it startled her.

Suddenly her frozen limbs worked again. She stood on tiptoe and stared out the window. She could see nothing, hear nothing. It was as if the beast had disappeared.

"Atalanta," her father called.

Running over to him, she fell to her knees by his pallet. "What is it, Papa?"

"Is it . . ." he whispered with difficulty. "Is it . . . gone?"

"I don't know, Papa," she said, her voice almost as weak as his. "But I wounded it. I stuck my knife in its paw. Through the window."

"Wounded badly?" His words were so quiet, she had to bend over and put her ear close to his mouth.

She shook her head. "I'm not certain. But the knife was still in when it backed away."

He managed to sit up. "You need to find out. We cannot leave it wounded." He coughed, an awful frothy sound. "Take the small spear. But for Artemis' sake, be careful." He fell back.

"I will, Papa." She knew a wounded beast could be even more dangerous.

Going over to the corner by the door, she fetched her father's short spear where it was propped beside their nets and snares. Carefully, she slid the beam from the door, then stood for a long moment listening for any hint of danger.

It was quiet outside.

Perhaps, she thought, *too quiet.* But she went out anyway. She had no other choice.

CHAPTER TWO

THE RING

A talanta kept the wall of the house to her back for protection. Step-by-step she edged her way around the cottage, spear point raised to meet any sudden attack.

Large footprints, one of them outlined in blood, led from the window. Four great claw marks were gouged out of the door.

The footprints led to the middle of the clearing and then—impossibly—vanished.

She found her knife lying on the grass, a streak of dark blood staining the blade. Picking it up, she saw a tuft of orange fur sticking to it.

"So . . ." she whispered. "You pulled the knife out with your teeth. Smart boy." She stuck the bit of fur down the front of her tunic and glanced quickly around the clearing. The sun was about gone. It would be too dangerous to remain outside in the dark.

As soon as she returned to the cottage, Atalanta set the bar across the door again.

"Not there," she told her father. "Not anywhere."

He nodded. "Now you must tend my wound, child."

She felt tears start in her eyes, hot and prickly. "You'll be fine, Papa. I'll take care of you."

First she built up the fire, for he was shivering with cold. Then she began to wash and dress the wound with folded lengths of sheepskin. But no matter how many bandages she wrapped around his side, the blood still seeped through.

Her father didn't stop her. Her touch seemed to soothe him.

"What sort of beast was it, Papa?" she asked in a trembling voice. The tip of her dark braid was now sticky with his blood. "I saw a back as high as the window, a paw with claws like a mountain cat's, but bigger."

The huntsman shook his head, shutting his eyes tight against a surge of pain. "I don't know." He took a deep breath. "Perhaps it's some beast migrating from one land to another and only passing through Arcadia. It must have come upon us by accident."

Pulling the hank of orange fur from her tunic, she showed it to her father. In the firelight, it looked flecked with gold. "Look what I found, Papa."

He touched the fur with a stained finger. "This is my last trophy."

She didn't tell him it was *her* knife that had cut that swatch.

He coughed, a thread of blood sliding from the side of his mouth into his white-streaked beard. "Whatever it is, the creature has dealt me my death blow."

The tuft of fur dropped from his feeble fingers.

"Papa!" she whispered. He didn't answer, but she could tell by the rattle of his breath that he was not asleep.

She added more wood to the fire till the room was uncomfortably warm. Then she made him a tisane of heal-all, feeding it to him as if he were a baby, using a leather bottle and a cloth teat. After that he dozed until midnight.

When he woke, he whispered hoarsely, "I'm dying, Atalanta." His watery eyes were the color of an autumn sky.

"No, Papa, no," Atalanta cried. But looking down at him, she knew he was telling the truth.

"You must be a brave girl," he said.

When had he become so small? she wondered. All her life he'd seemed tree high, a big man, striding ahead of her in the woods, following tracks and spoor as surely as if they were signs engraved in stone. He could throw his javelin with deadly accuracy across the widest glade. The arrows leaped from his bow like hawks taking flight. As his only child, she'd always been his constant companion, learning all the lore of the forest at his side.

But since her mother's death three years earlier, he'd seemed to shrink a little every day. And now, coughing out specks of blood, he was scarcely her own size.

He struggled to sit up in the bed and she helped him. "But I must tell you now how you came to us," he said. "I'll not die until you know it all." He coughed again, groaned, and the wound seeped like a bog.

Atalanta shook her head "Do not speak, Papa, it wearies you."

"You must know."

"I know you found me in the woods, Papa, when I was four years old."

"Found you by a great she-bear who was long dead," he said between coughs.

She brushed his thin fair hair back from his forehead. The skin was burning hot, his blue eyes cloudy.

"I know, Papa."

"And you covered with bites, some . . ." He bent over with the coughing and she held him till he was done.

"Some long healed and some quite new," she whispered. It was a story they had often told together. "I know, Papa."

"You were like a wild thing yourself," her father resumed. "Abandoned on Mount Parthenon by uncaring parents and by some miracle of the gods suckled by that she-bear for who knows how long. How slowly I had to approach you, how softly I had to speak to keep you from fleeing."

"It was only by luring me on with food that you were able to make me follow you," Atalanta continued for him as he stopped to suck in a few last breaths.

"And I brought you home to Mama who wanted a child and had none." His voice faltered twice, on "Mama" and on "none." He caught himself, then said, "A miracle of the gods she called it. How else would a wild beast give life to a helpless baby? I told her that most likely one of the she-bear's cubs had been stillborn so that she accepted a human child in its place." It was the most he had spoken since getting his wound. The speaking had exhausted him and he fell forward.

Atalanta caught him and rocked him as if he were a child. She knew the story, even though her own memory of the events was dim. When her father had found her, she couldn't even speak, only growl and snap like an animal. She had run about on all fours. Had eaten raw meat. Perhaps—she thought—perhaps it was because she had no words to form her memory of those early days that all she could recall was the sharp smell of the old she-bear, the warmth of the fur when she pressed her face into it, the rough-and-tumble company of the cubs who suckled at her side.

She patted her father's hand. "It doesn't matter now, Papa."

Her father sat up, eyes now shining brightly with the fever. "But it *does* matter. There is one thing you don't know, my daughter. And you *are* my daughter, for all that you were born elsewhere."

She would humor him and then maybe he would sleep again.

"What don't I know, Papa."

He reached a trembling hand beneath the pallet and pulled out a leather pouch. "Open it. I can't . . ."

She took the pouch, pulled it open, drew out a signet ring.

"This ring was strung on a leather thong around your neck."

She held the ring up to the flickering light of the hearth fire. On the stone was an engraving of a great boar.

Her father whispered weakly, "I kept that from you all these years. I was afraid, you see, that you would seek out your real father and leave me."

"*You* are my real father, Papa," Atlanta whispered, setting the ring aside. But she spoke to a dead man.

CHAPTER THREE

BURYING THE PAST

W hen Atalanta woke in the morning, she was by her father's side. For a moment she wondered why he seemed so cold, and then she remembered and wept again.

This time she wept not for him—he looked so peaceful now and free of pain—but for herself. She shook with the spasms and cried out loud. There was no one left to tell her to be brave.

At last, exhausted by all the weeping, she rubbed the tears from her eyes. Then hefting the spear and taking the knife as well, she went outside.

The tracks of the night before were undisturbed and there seemed no new ones, which was a relief. She crouched down to examine them carefully this time.

"I don't understand," she whispered, for the tracks were very puzzling. They looked something like a mountain cat's, only twice the size. The toes were more widely spread, which meant they supported a heavier body. Also the weight seemed concentrated on the front paws, which was not how a cat walked.

She followed the tracks around the house to the window where she had knifed the beast. There was a dark stain on the sill and down the side of the wall. The bloodstains led directly to the clearing where the creature had taken the knife from its paw. And here was the greatest mystery of all, which she had only guessed at the night before. The paw prints simply disappeared.

This time she looked around carefully. The closest tree was surely too far away for the animal to have jumped to. So were the rocks. Yet that was surely what had happened—rock or tree. The soft earth of the clearing showed nothing more.

Atalanta tried to puzzle it out the way her father had taught her. If the beast leaped, with a wounded paw, did he do it to hide his trail? If so, she knew, he was very intelligent.

Big.

Fierce.

Intelligent.

She shook her head. It was the worst of all combinations.

By the time the sun was high, and she had not heard or seen anything more of the beast, Atalanta decided to go to the stream for a basin of water, but she carried her spear, knife in her belt, just in case.

It seemed unnaturally quiet by the water, as if the whole clearing knew of her father's death and every bird, every little animal, was still in his honor.

"Thank you," she whispered to the woods about her. Then she brought back a basin full of water to wash her father's body in preparation for burying him.

Her grief had passed for the present. She would not let it return until she had done her duty.

Resting the flint shovel and the spear on her shoulder, she walked out behind the humble dwelling to where a mound of rocks marked where her mother was buried. Choosing a spot to the left of the simple marker, she anchored the spear, haft end down in the grass, where it would be close at hand should she need it. Then she stabbed the blade of the shovel into the ground and ripped up a tussock of grass and earth.

Soon a heap of earth was piled up at her side and sweat flowed down her face as freely as tears.

Her arms ached with the strain, but she had to keep digging. Having helped bury her mother, she knew that it was important to dig the grave quickly and pile rocks atop. Here in the heart of the forest, death was a lure to creatures both great and small who wished to eat without the bother of having to kill.

At last she stood, red-faced and panting, by the side of the open pit. Now came a harder task. She walked back into the cottage, all the while fighting down the small voice of hope.

Perhaps he's just sleeping, said that deceptive voice. *When you go inside he'll be there as usual, his strong arms open to greet you.* But he lay just as she had left him after she'd washed away the dark blood.

Shrunken as he was, he was still too heavy for her to carry. Instead she hooked her hands under his arms and dragged him wrapped in his blanket across the earthen floor and out onto the grass where her spear stood sentinel. There, with one last effort, she rolled her father into the open grave.

Looking down at his still form tangled in the blanket, she wanted to speak to him, wanted to tell him she was trying to be brave. Instead she bit her lip.

No, she thought, *words will lead to tears and there is no time for more tears.*

She drew herself up wearily and began shoveling the loose earth over her father's body. Slowly it disappeared from view.

Where is he now? Atalanta wondered. *A sad shade drifting like smoke through the lightless passageways of the Underworld? Or has he found a route to the Elysian Fields where the blessed souls pass their days in eternal sunshine?* She hoped he was there, in Elysia, just on the edge of a little woods because she could not imagine him living forever without a forest to walk in.

She suddenly remembered Papa offering a prayer to the gods to guide and protect Mama on her journey. Atalanta rubbed her sweaty brow. What were their names again? Papa and Mama hadn't invoked the gods very often, here in their woods.

Then she remembered. There was Demeter, goddess of the earth. And Artemis, goddess of the hunt. Papa always called Atalanta his little Artemis. And Pan, the goat-footed god of beasts and herders. That exhausted her memory.

"Demeter . . . Artemis . . . Pan." How strange the words sounded coming from her lips. "Take care of my papa. Let there be trees and quiet streams where he is now."

She couldn't think of anything else to say. How could the gods hear her anyway? If they lived at all, it was in some far-off place. She doubted any of them ever visited Arcadia.

Her eyes rested on the freshly dug earth and, for a moment, she had a brief memory of her father striding ahead of her through the trees, full of strength and confidence.

"He *is* in the Elysian Fields," she told herself. "With Mama."

She would believe that always.

As she began to gather the memorial stones, she had

a sudden thought: *They'll have each other. And I . . . I am now utterly alone. It will be years before I am with them again.* She couldn't think of any way to cure that. Not tears, certainly. If she killed the beast, would that still the pain in her heart?

But surely, she thought, *the beast is long gone from here.*

Just then there was a loud sound behind her, in the bushes by the side of the cottage, as if something were ripping its way toward her.

She sprang up in a fighting position, grabbing up the spear and holding it pointed at the greenery. The creature was between her and the cottage. She would have to fight it with the spear and knife. *And the shovel, too, if necessary.*

Suddenly the bushes parted, and a great brown bear twice her size reared up before her.

Atalanta took a startled step back, and the beast dashed the spear from her hands with a mighty sweep of its paw. The impact knocked her to the ground and winded her. Before she could make another move, the bear pinned her down, its round hairy face blocking out the sky, the wide maw parting to expose long wicked teeth. Its breath was awful, like an opened grave, and the vast jaws descended upon her.

Atalanta shut her eyes against the horror. *Papa,* she thought, *I will be with you sooner than I expected.*

CHAPTER FOUR

URSO

T he very last thing she ever expected to happen happened. Her skull was not crushed by a killing blow; her throat was not ripped open by those savage teeth.

Instead she felt the bear's tongue rasp wetly across her cheek.

Slowly she opened her eyes. The bear's head still loomed over her, its mouth wide open. But there was no flash of hunger or rage in his bright eyes.

Instead they looked . . . friendly.

His muzzle came down and his black nose nuzzled against her ear. Then he released her and rolled over on the grass, waving his paws playfully.

Atalanta sat up and at once the bear rolled back to

her, pressing his snout against her ribs.

Hesitantly, she reached out and rubbed her fingers in the warm fur of his neck. Something about this set up a tingling at the back of her mind. It was all so familiar: the strong, musky animal smell; the roughness of the fur beneath her hand; the sound of the bear's grunting as it turned from one side to the other.

She reached way back into her memory, and suddenly as if in a dream, she saw herself—small and dirty, growling and snapping like an animal—rolling across the grass with a bear cub. They bared teeth and cuffed one another, but none of it was meant to hurt. It was all in play.

Then she remembered something else—that bear cub had a large ragged piece missing from his left ear, from an encounter with an angry wildcat.

She pulled the great head down toward her and examined his left ear. There was a ragged piece missing.

This *had* to be her old playmate grown large. He must have recognized her smell, just as she knew him from the tear in his ear.

A sudden awful thought occurred to her. What if he were the very beast that had killed her father?

The bear nuzzled her once more and she laughed at her own fears. The death creature had orange hair. The tuft was still in the cabin, near her father's pallet.

Scratching the bear behind his mutilated ear, she whispered, "So, old boy, we have certainly changed from our cub days, you and I."

The bear tossed his head and barked in response.

Atalanta pushed him onto his back and rubbed his big soft belly, thinking that it was good to be alive after all. It was good not to be abandoned. She had lost mother and father. But she had gained a . . . brother.

"I wonder what brought you here now?" Atalanta asked, still stroking the bear's fur. She was careful to keep her voice low and soothing. "Because if you had been here for a while, my father would surely have hunted you down." A bear would have meant meat for the winter, a fur mantle for them both, and teeth and bone for jewelry to trade at the market.

The bear rolled over and raked a row of furrows in the earth with one big paw.

Atalanta smiled at him. "I expect you are just lonely. No mother. No father. No sisters or brothers. No mate. So you let your nose find your old littermate."

The bear sat up. He looked a little foolish, his tongue lolling out.

"There's something out there that killed my papa," she said, standing. "Something big. Something awful. With orange fur and claws that can deliver a death wound. I'm sure it's still around here and I have to find it. For my papa's sake. Will you come, too?"

Almost as if he understood her, the bear gave a grunt and stood up, padding after her to the cottage door. He sniffed loudly but would not cross the threshold.

Going inside without him, Atalanta turned. "I'll just

get my things," she said, leaving the door open so he could see what she was doing.

Pausing in the middle of the room, Atalanta took a deep breath. Memories filled every corner: the smell of her mother's freshly baked bread, the sharp scent of a clutch of fish hung up to smoke in the hearth. Here was the doll her mother had fashioned for her with a walnut for a face and dried rushes for hair. Here was the little skull of the first rabbit she had shot with her bow. Her father had set it proudly over the hearth as a trophy and there it had remained. Here was her mother's loom, the *peplos* half woven and left there to gather dust.

Best to be away from here and forget, she decided suddenly. *From now on home is wherever I choose to be.*

She took a pouch and filled it with dried fruit, olives, and apples. Then she filled a water skin from the big earthenware jar in the corner. Folding an extra wool cloak over her arm, she slung her bow and arrows over her back. Finally she stuck a gutting knife in her belt and picked up her javelin, the knotty ash handle well worn from her days of practice with her father.

As an afterthought, she stuffed the tuft of orange hair down the front of her garment. It was scratchy and stank.

She was just about to leave the cottage when her eye caught something glinting on the floor beside the bloodstained pallet.

The signet ring!

Crouching down, she picked it up between two fingers, examining it as if it were the spoor of an animal.

Can this guide me back to my other father? she wondered. *To the one who lost me?*

She hung the ring around her neck on a leather cord and, for a moment, pressed it against her chest. But only for a moment. She had other business to tend to. It was not her past she was hunting, but the creature who had slain her father.

The bear suddenly poked his muzzle through the open doorway, sniffing warily.

"There's nothing for you here, boy," Atalanta told him. "Nothing for me anymore either." She pushed past him, then walked outside, closing the door behind.

With the bear ambling by her side, Atalanta set off for the woods.

"The orange beast," she told the bear, "vanished from the clearing. Perhaps it has gone back to where we first came upon it—the spring." It was a guess only. She had nothing else. "Maybe it's got a lair nearby."

The bear growled as if offering help.

Well, he might be useful, Atalanta thought. *He has a good nose.* She had the tuft of hair to let him smell.

Besides, without the bear at her side, would she have the courage to face whatever was out there? Most likely she'd be curled up in the cottage, nursing her misery like a wound.

"Bear . . ." she began, then stopped. "If we're going to be partners, I need to call you something."

The bear waited patiently for her to continue.

Atalanta thought for a while. She'd never needed much in the way of names before. "Papa" and "Mama" were all she'd ever used.

"Urso," she declared at last, turning to look directly at the bear, for *this* matter of a name suddenly seemed important. "Urso. That sounds like a fine bear's name to me. How does it sound to you?"

The bear sat up on his hind legs and clapped his paws together with a strange clacketing sound as his nails hit against one another.

"I thought you'd like it," Atalanta said, and grinned.

Urso grinned back, showing two rows of very large teeth.

Atalanta appreciated those teeth. "Now," she said, "let's get on with the hunt."

CHAPTER FIVE

ON THE TRACK

A s soon as she reached the spring, Atalanta felt a tingle of alarm run down her back. Could the beast be here, lying in wait? She knew it was intelligent.

Intelligent enough to set a trap?

She held her breath and listened. All she could hear was Urso, snuffling and pawing at the ground beside her. Her stomach lurched sickeningly and a hot flush spread over her face. The urge to run away was almost overwhelming.

Urso rubbed his muzzle consolingly against her back.

"You're right, Urso," she agreed, looking over her shoulder at him. "I *have* to do this."

Gripping her javelin firmly in both hands, she

stepped into the shadow of the greenery. Snapped branches and mashed ferns marked the beast's passage, but there was nothing to show if the tracks were old or new.

"We can backtrack him," she told the bear. "Maybe find where he came from."

The bear went ahead, sniffing out the way. Where the trees thinned out on the other side, she found a jumble of footprints.

Urso made a low, unhappy growl at the back of his throat. Like all bears, he had a muscular hump on his back just below the neck, and the hairs on it were standing straight up.

"You smell something you don't like," Atalanta said.

Urso stood up on his hind legs and whined.

Reaching into her shirt, Atalanta drew out the tuft of orange hair, shoving it under his nose. "Here. Is this what you smell?"

The bear grabbed up the tuft of hair in his mouth and shook his head back and forth with such ferocity, he looked as if he were going to shake himself in two. Then suddenly he dropped the orange tuft to the ground, turned around, and urinated on it.

"Uck," Atalanta cried. There was no way she would pick up the tuft now and shove it down the front of her shirt. But that didn't matter. Urso was clearly furious that the creature had invaded their forest.

"Come," she said to the bear, and bending low, she

followed the tracks for another hundred feet.

Once again, the prints just stopped.

Jamming her spear point into the ground, Atalanta paused to take a swallow from her water skin. "I don't understand," she said. "This creature seems to appear out of thin air and then disappear again, just as it pleases."

A sudden rustling in the branches behind put her immediately on alert. Urso bared his teeth.

Carefully, Atalanta lowered the water skin and slid the bow from her shoulder. Then in one quick movement she fitted an arrow to her bowstring. Spinning about, she loosed off a shot. The arrow clipped the bushy tail of a squirrel, sending it chittering into cover.

Atalanta gave herself a slap on the leg, partly for being so foolish but mostly for missing the target. What would Papa have said if he'd seen her waste an arrow like that? Probably, *Think, Atalanta—a good hunter's most useful weapon is the brain.*

She looked until she found the arrow, buried lightly in the trunk of an oak that was twisted with the silvered leaves of an ivy vine. Pulling the arrow out carefully, she checked to be certain that the arrowhead was still whole before smoothing its feathers and replacing it in her quiver.

She shook her head. "That's it, then, bear. We're going to have to search the whole forest."

He grunted in return.

They searched for the rest of the day without finding any more tracks. Not the beast's trail—nor any deer's or boar's trail either. Atalanta knew she was a good stalker. Her father had boasted to the hunters they occasionally met that she was the most natural trail-finder he'd ever known.

But there was nothing.

Nothing!

The longer they searched, the more Atalanta worried. The beast was huge and smart, and she feared he might be invisible as well. Even if they found the thing, she wondered if she was strong enough to kill it, with or without Urso's help.

Urso seemed baffled, too. He made curious little snuffling sounds, and more than once simply sat down in the middle of the path, as if to say he wasn't going a step farther.

By early evening Atalanta was beginning to think about finding a campsite.

"A cave," she said to the bear. That would be more easily defended than an open clearing.

Urso was walking ahead of her when all of a sudden he crouched low, his back hump bristling. He began to growl.

She ran over and put her hand on his back, whispering, "What do you smell?" Her fingers tightened around the haft of the javelin. "Is it the beast?"

Urso started forward through the bushes and Atalanta followed close behind. The bushes snapped back against her bare legs but she never noticed. She was intent on what was ahead.

They entered a small clearing. It was filled with the stink of recent death, a day or two old at the most. Flies buzzed around a corpse. Or what was left of one. It was clearly a deer, a big stag by the antlers. But the rest had been stripped, flesh and innards devoured, bones scattered. Only a few tatters of brown skin were left, some dangling from branches of a tall tree. It was around those tatters that the flies were buzzing.

Urso growled, long and low.

"What *is* this creature?" Atalanta whispered. She had never seen such a kill before. The deer had simply been ripped to pieces. And there were no tracks leading to or away from the place.

None.

They found a nearby cave and once Urso had sniffed it out, declaring it safe, they sheltered there for the night. He slept by the entrance, filling the opening with his big furry presence.

Atalanta put her head against his flank, using it as a kind of pillow. With each breath the bear took, his body rose and fell beneath her head. After the grief of the day, she was happy to be lulled to sleep that way.

Her last dreaming thought was that tomorrow would bring the start of a new life. A life in the wild. Or maybe, she thought—remembering the bear that had mothered her—maybe it was a return to her old one. Either way, she promised herself she would be ready.

CHAPTER SIX

THE WOODLAND GOD

The beast's trail was not to be found. For days the two of them hunted for it, casting larger and larger circles with the deer's few pitiful remains as the center of their search.

They returned each night to the cave that had become their home.

For the first few days, the search was all that had mattered. But as it became clear the beast had really disappeared, the two of them began to enjoy sharing the wild together. They chased through the trees, splashed happily in the streams, found wild berries and sweet honey, and ate fish the bear caught in his big claws. He even learned to like the fish cooked over an oak fire, for Atalanta could not stand eating it raw.

However, one morning when Atalanta woke, Urso was not in the cave.

She got up slowly, stretched, poked her head out of the cave entrance, thinking he was off fishing on his own.

"Urso," she called.

There was no low growling answer.

"Are you hiding?"

Still no response.

Taking her javelin and knife and water skin, she went down to the river. She checked their berry bushes, their honey tree, even tracked halfway back to the deer clearing.

There was no sign of him.

So she did what she should have done at first, *would* have done at first if she'd not been in such a hurry: follow his trail from the cave.

He'd made no attempt to disguise his tracks. They led north.

"Now why are you going there?" she whispered. She was resolved to follow him. But something stopped her, something her father had once said about male bears. "They are solitary creatures."

Well, he hadn't been solitary in the past week.

She thought about that. Perhaps he had done that for her, to help her, his old littermate. But now he needed time to himself.

Sitting on her haunches, Atalanta stared northward. "You'll return, bear," she whispered. "When you're ready." She was sure of it.

But now, for the first time, she felt truly alone. She tried the word out loud. "Alone." It was less frightening that way. *"Alone!"*

Actually, she'd never had much to do with people. Never really wanted to. Her mother and father and the forest had been enough for her.

Oh, once in a while her father brought home hunters he knew who were in their woods. Sometimes she'd accompanied him when he went on a trading journey to the villages of the Arcadian plain. There they'd bartered deerskins, rabbit pelts, tusks and antlers for corn, cheese, olives, wine. He seemed at ease with the villagers, bantering back and forth with them.

But on those visits, when she'd stood in the market-place, Atalanta had been aware of the stares she drew— from children and adults alike. Somehow they could sense her wildness and wanted no part of it. Many were the fights she'd gotten into, wiping the smirk from a mocking face with a slap from the butt end of her small spear. No matter how outnumbered she was, she always held her own—kicking and clawing like a crazed wildcat.

"There'd be no trouble if they'd only leave me alone," she'd told her father. "All I want is to be left alone."

"You're too wild, daughter," he told her.

"I like being wild."

She thought about the villages now.

"I can manage just fine out here," she told herself.

"They have nothing I need. Nothing."

But she missed the bear.

Urso was away for almost a week before returning.

The second time he left, Atalanta was anxious about it, but by the third time, she understood his pattern and was comfortable with it.

Each time they came together again, it was a grand reunion. They would seek out rivers and pools where they plunged under the water with a huge splash to see who could come up with the biggest fish. They ran races through the twisting forest tracks, Atalanta forcing her legs to move faster and faster until she could just about keep pace with Urso as he bounded along.

They no longer looked for the killer beast. It was gone as if it had never been.

One day when Urso was off by himself, Atalanta spent the morning weaving a vine rope to hang over their favorite pool as a swing. She'd gotten about three body lengths done and was just casting about for some more vines. Suddenly, an odd whistling sounded across the river, like lark song, only longer, more elaborate.

Atalanta rose and waded into the water, following the stream of notes as if enchanted. Climbing up the far embankment, she found herself in a strange glade. In the shade of a leafy oak stood a grotesque figure, part man, part animal.

His face was brown and wrinkled, like an apple too long in the sun. He had thick, sensual lips, a sharp nose with wide nostrils. His arms and chest were matted with dark curling hair. As she got closer, she could see that a pair of small, sharp horns rose out of his thatch of thick brown curls. Most surprising of all were his legs. They were like those of a goat; instead of feet, he had hooves.

The whistling came from a set of reed pipes the strange creature was playing with his eyes closed. As if he knew she was there, he stopped playing, opened his eyes, and smiled.

"Ah, Atalanta, the little huntress," he said, letting the pipes dangle from a cord around his neck. His voice was unexpectedly low and lilting. "I wondered when I'd run into you."

For one shocking moment, Atalanta wondered if he might be the very creature who killed her father. But as quickly, she realized he had no huge claws, no orange fur. Strange as he was, he was not the beast.

"How . . ." she began before her voice cracked. She tried again. "How do you know me?"

He broke into a laugh that was like water over stone. "I know all sorts of things."

She hated to be laughed at and said angrily, "Who are you? Why are you in my forest?"

"*Your* forest?" He laughed again.

"Mine and the bear's," she said stubbornly.

His face softened. "Mine, too," he said. "I'm the god

of this woodland. Your people call me Pan."

"I don't have any people," she answered. "Not any-more. There's just me."

"I am sorry for that," he said, his voice low.

It was the tone of it, with its hint of human comfort, that broke her. She could feel herself starting to cry. *Once started,* she thought, *and I'll never stop.* Instead, she forced herself to say, "You're a real god? I've never seen a god before."

He grinned at her.

Putting her head to one side, she considered him. "You're not very impressive."

"I could say the same about you," Pan replied, "but I'm in the mood to be charming. When I'm charming, I'm irresistible." He laughed again.

The sound shivered down Atalanta's spine, but deli-ciously.

"See," Pan said, "you are liking me already."

"I am not."

"Are, too."

Really, she thought, *he is more like a child than a man. That's the way I used to argue with Papa when I was younger.* Thinking of her father brought a wave of sadness.

As if sensing her pain, Pan asked immediately, "What's wrong? Can I help?"

She looked at him and thought that if he was really a god of the woodland, perhaps he knew something about the beast. She asked, "Tell me what creature slew my father. Where is it? How can I find it?"

Pan gave a dismissive wave with his hand and kicked the grass with one hoof. "I am no oracle. And I certainly will not help you seek out a beast for vengeance."

"You asked me what help you could be and I told you," Atalanta said.

"That's *not* why I am here." Pan looked at her with mischievous eyes.

"Then why *are* you here?"

He smiled and spread his arms wide apart. "To discover why you are in my realm."

"I live here," she said.

"The birds and the rabbits, the fish and the otters are all part of my domain," he said. "The deer and the boar and the bear." His hooves drummed on the ground. "And of course the goats!"

She waited, hands on her hips.

"But *you* are not one of my creatures," Pan said. "You belong with your own kind."

"My kind threw me out when I was an infant. I was nursed by a bear. The only humans who loved me were my adopted papa and mama, and they are both dead."

Pan nodded but said nothing.

"The bear Urso is my friend and companion. He cares for me. So who do *you* think are my kind?" Atalanta could feel her cheeks flaming.

"Humans can be friends with wild folk. Indeed, I

encourage it. Nevertheless, that does not make them kin. Atalanta, you are a human and not a beast," Pan said.

Atalanta shrugged. "I can't help that."

Pan's eyes gleamed. "But I can." He made a gesture with his left hand and suddenly a pomegranate appeared in his palm. He stretched out his arm, offering the fruit to Atalanta. "One bite and you'll turn into any kind of animal you choose."

She put her hand out to take the fruit, then pulled back. "That's not possible."

"Everything is possible for the gods," Pan said. He leaned toward her, the pomegranate tantalizingly close. "You could be a doe, a sow, even a she-bear. Isn't that what you want?"

Atalanta looked down at herself, at her clever hands, her quick feet. She hugged herself, feeling her humanity. "I'm not . . . not sure," she said.

"Not sure you want to be an animal?" he asked, stepping closer to her. "Or not sure you want to be a human?" A thick odor of musk wafted from his shaggy body.

For a moment Atalanta wanted to scream and run from him. She fought down the panic and stared back. "Not sure," she said stubbornly.

He grinned. "What have you got to lose? Nothing but troublesome thoughts and pointless questions. Things the forest creatures never worry about."

She leaned away from him. Really, the smell was overpowering. Not like Urso at all, but rank and enticing at the same time. "What do you mean—troublesome thoughts and pointless questions?"

He withdrew the pomegranate, holding it close to his chest. "Oh, you know—thoughts like *Where do I come from? What's going to become of me?* All that nonsense."

Atalanta's hand drifted to the ring about her neck. She thought: *Where* do *I come from? What* is *going to become of me?* And then she wondered: *Would I really prefer not to have those kinds of thoughts?*

"And then," Pan continued, as if guessing what she was thinking, "there are the bad memories. Your mother's long sickness. Your father's awful death."

"How do you know . . ." she began.

He took a bite of the pomegranate himself, letting the juice run down his chin. "All that pain will be forgotten with a single bite." He thrust the fruit under her nose, grinning broadly and revealing two rows of crooked teeth.

"Forget Mama? Forget Papa?" Atalanta said, the breath whooshing out of her. "Never!"

"Never?"

"I'll live with Urso in the wild just as I am."

"Really?" Pan said. He threw the pomegranate into the air and caught it between his thumb and forefinger. "It's not all that easy, child. The lure of one's own kind is hard to resist."

"I thought . . ." Atalanta said, this time leaning toward him, "I thought you said you weren't an oracle."

Pan shrugged his hairy shoulders. Then he threw the pomegranate into the air again. This time it did not come down. "You don't understand," he said. "But then mortals never do. That's what makes them such delightful fools."

He turned and, playing his pipes once again, disappeared as if the air had swallowed him.

Atalanta was left, gaping.

And alone once more.

CHAPTER SEVEN

THE TRAP

It was another five days before Urso returned, and by then the meeting with Pan had become a half-remembered dream. Once Atalanta tried to tell the bear what she could recall of it—something about the lure of her own kind—but for some reason, her tongue refused to speak of it.

She simply put her arms around the bear's shaggy neck. "You are my kin and my kind now," she told him.

He answered by licking her face with his tongue, his breath strong and familiar.

As the weeks with Urso went by, Atalanta learned how to fish like a bear, standing still in the water and then snatching a glistening silver body out with a quick scoop of her hands. She learned as well how to raid the honey-bee's hive and how to strip a berry bush bare. The palms of her hands became hardened and stained.

She taught Urso how to play hide-and-find, something she and her father had enjoyed. It quickly became the bear's favorite game.

One day, as the two of them were playing, it was Urso's turn to hide. Finding him was not difficult. Atalanta knew his tracks and scent too well for long concealment. And he always seemed to hide in the same places. Still, as if playing with a small child, Atalanta could stretch the game out for hours.

This time she found him near their den. She leaned forward to tap him on the nose—a signal that she'd won.

He rolled away from her and she leaped onto his back, trying to reach a hand to his muzzle.

Shaking her off, he made a low, pleasant grumbling sound, which she'd come to know as his teasing sound. Then he bounded off toward the trees.

"You don't get away that easily, you big ball of fur!" she cried, getting up and racing after him. She leaped over rocks and roots and was just about to grab him by the tail when something astonishing happened.

He disappeared into the earth as though a giant maw had swallowed him.

Atalanta tumbled headlong after him, bounced off his back, and rolled to a stop against the side of an enormous hole, twice as high as her head and big enough for two bears.

Struggling groggily to her feet, Atalanta was relieved to find she'd broken no bones. However, her bow had snapped in two under the impact. Tossing the broken weapon aside, she knelt beside Urso and rubbed her face against his neck.

"Are you all right?" she asked.

A deep rumble vibrated in his throat. Slowly he rose onto three paws, holding his right forward paw up as if it hurt.

Atalanta felt the paw. "No bones broken. But if it hurts, it's going to make it harder for you to get out of here." She looked around the hole. It was clearly not a natural trough in the earth, for there were signs of digging along the steep, sheer sides. About them lay the broken remnants of a lattice of leaves and branches that had concealed the opening till Urso's weight had crashed through.

"It's a trap, Urso," she said. Then remembering something her father had told her about such hunting pits, she added, "Lucky there were no sharpened stakes at the bottom."

The bear growled his answer.

Atalanta thought that—given time—she might be able to use her arrowheads to gouge out a series of hand and footholds into the earth wall. But how long would that take?

"And when will the hunters come to check their trap?" she asked the bear.

He shook his massive head.

"Maybe . . ." she told him, staring up at the opening above them, "maybe there's a faster way out." She calculated the height. "Come here. Stand on your hind legs. Like this."

It took a moment to coax him, a moment to explain. She pressed her belly against the earth wall, standing as tall as she could, arms stretched above her head. Urso at last understood and reared up beside her, bracing his left forepaw against the side of the pit.

She clambered up his shaggy back and placed her feet on his shoulders. Then she strained upward until her arms ached, but her fingers were barely brushing the lip of the pit.

"Sorry, Urso," she called down to him. She placed one foot on his head. "This is the only way."

She let herself stand there for a mere moment before she threw an elbow over the edge of the hole and dragged herself up the rest of the way, her toes getting but small purchase on the side of the pit. Finally, with a squeal of triumph, she rolled away from the pit's edge and lay on her back, gasping.

When she'd caught her breath, she leaned back over the pit. "I'm going to find something to get you out of there, Urso. Don't worry." Though she herself was panicked.

She knew there was rope back at her father's house, but that was an hour's run at least. She doubted they had that much time. And anyway, the bear's claws could not cling to a rope the way a pair of hands could. Especially if he'd injured one of them.

"Not a rope, then," she told herself. "What else?" She rose and went into the trees, hoping for inspiration.

Then she saw it—a fallen tree trunk, the insides of which had been eaten out by insects.

"A ladder," she whispered. *If* it would bear Urso's weight.

She put her hands under the trunk and pushed. Even hollowed out it was still quite a weight. She had to rock it back and forth till it came loose from the earth that seemed to hold it. But at last she managed to roll it— slowly and with much effort—to the edge of the pit.

Now all she had to do was maneuver it carefully into position.

She leaned over. "Urso!" she called down.

The bear had already been alerted by the sounds of the tree trunk being rolled. He was up on his hind legs.

Atalanta motioned to him with her hand. "Move to one side. I'm going to slide this log down so you can climb up."

He seemed to understand and crouched along the far side of the pit.

Then slowly, carefully, she tilted the log over the edge, holding on to it long enough to guide it as it slid into the hole. Luckily the end struck the bottom and seemed to fix there, leaving the rest to lean against the side of the pit. It did not reach all the way to the top but would take Urso more than halfway. And halfway was all he would need.

The bear walked along the side of the log and sniffed at it, as if calculating whether it would carry his weight.

"Come on, you slowpoke, hurry. There's no knowing when that hunter will return." Though she suspected it was more than one. One person could not have dug that hole—or expect to get a bear out of it.

Urso started to climb, limping whenever he had to put pressure on the injured paw.

"You can do it," Atalanta called.

He growled and kept moving.

Suddenly they heard a distant sound. For a moment they both froze.

"Wrong way, Goryx!" a voice called. "The pit's over here."

"I don't think so," came the rough answer. "I recognize this rock."

A third voice laughed. "That's because it reminds you of your own thick head!"

Atalanta unfroze first. "Hurry, Urso!" she cried in a desperate whisper. "The hunters!"

Urso had managed only a few feet, for every three inches forward, he seemed to slip back two.

It was clear to Atalanta that he wouldn't make it out.

Not in the time they had left.

"I'll get you *more* time," she told him, and stood. "You just keep climbing. Then run away from here, as fast as you can." Fingering the knife at her belt, she looked toward the path where the voices were coming from. She hadn't been able to save her father, but she was certainly going to save her brother-bear.

CHAPTER EIGHT

THE HUNTERS

C rouching low, Atalanta glided silently through the forest. She could hear the hunters coming closer.

"We wouldn't be having this trouble if we'd stuck to our usual hunting grounds," complained the grating voice, Goryx.

"We wouldn't have come this far if the game weren't so scarce," another reminded him.

Atalanta buried herself in some blueberry bushes and listened to the men's footsteps padding along the path. Carefully she peered through the leaves, thinking that they were not very good hunters, making all that noise.

There were three of them, armed with daggers and

spears. Ropes and snares hung from their belts. That weighted down, they would not go fast.

Good, she thought. *Better for Urso.*

One of the men had a long face with a beaked nose. Another was shorter, squat, with a squashed face like a gourd left in the sun. The third had a dark scar down his right arm.

Scar was in the lead with Beak Nose bringing up the rear, grumbling to himself about his aching feet.

Atalanta let them pass her hiding place and then, when they were halfway around a bend in the path, she stood up and cupping her hands to her mouth, made loud growling noises.

The men stopped and turned, and she dropped back into the bushes.

"What was that?" came Goryx's grating voice.

"Doesn't sound like a bear," said Beak.

"More like a bear *cub*," Scar said.

Atalanta felt around her feet and picked up three rocks. *One for each of you,* she thought, waiting till they got closer. She listened for their footsteps, careful not to make the bushes tremble.

For hunters, they were terribly loud and she could hear them go past. The minute they were beyond her, she stood and tossed the rocks quickly, hitting them each on the back.

Then she dived back into the brush.

The hunters spun around with angry yells.

"What was that?" growled Goryx. "Somebody throwing rocks?"

"I don't see anybody," Beak Nose said. "Who'd be playing silly tricks like that so deep in the forest?"

"I'll wring their stupid necks if I catch them," Goryx threatened, rubbing the bruised spot on his back.

Scar raised a hand to silence them both. "Never mind that now. Stay alert. We need to move on and check the trap."

The other two grunted their agreement, and they started off again.

Atalanta realized that her plan to distract the men wasn't working, and Urso needed more time. Jumping out of cover with a whoop, she hurled herself at Beak Nose, landing heavily on his back and knocking him down. He shrieked, a sound as high and squealing as a pig in labor.

Scar grabbed her from behind and flung her to the ground, but she rolled nimbly to her feet and whipped out her knife. She didn't intend to hurt anyone, of course. Her plan was simply to give Urso more time to get out of the pit. But Scar didn't know that, and he raised his right arm to defend himself.

"Hold off, you little animal!" Goryx cried, grabbing her knife arm.

Atalanta turned her head and sank her teeth into the exposed skin of his wrist. He pulled away, cursing.

"Damned Amazon!" he cried.

From his knees, Beak Nose jammed his spear between Atalanta's feet and she stumbled back, losing her balance. She landed hard on her bottom and that gave Beak Nose a chance to catch her wrist and twist the knife from her grasp, tossing it way out of reach. In turn she kicked him hard in the shin with her sandal.

"By Hermes, she's a wild one!" he cried, backing away.

Shorty hefted his spear and was making ready to throw it at Atalanta, but Scar put up his hand. "No, Goryx—she's a child."

"Harpy's child most like," Goryx replied.

Atalanta made a sudden dive for her knife, but Scar had spotted her eyeing it. He reached out suddenly and grabbed her from behind and prisoned her arms against her sides.

Beak stared at her, taking in her torn and filthy clothing. "Look how skinny she is," he said. "She must be half crazed with hunger."

Scar laughed, and it rumbled against Atalanta's back. "You just like your women plump."

But Goryx was nodding his head. "She's crazy all right. Crazy mad. Like a dog with the foaming sickness."

"Don't just stand there gawping, Phreneus," Scar said, never slackening his grip on Atalanta's arms. "Use that leather cord of yours to tie her up before she does any more harm. How would we explain that at home? Three grown men bested by a child. And a girl at that."

Atalanta screeched in fury, but kick and wriggle as she might, she could not stop them winding the bonds around her arms and knotting them tightly. The scarred man continued to hold her as she fought in vain to free herself.

"There, that should do, Evenor," said Phreneus, regarding his work with pride.

"She's more beast than girl," said the squat Goryx. "Do you suppose she's a *maenad,* one of those mad-women who go dancing after the god Dionysus?"

"She's just a child who's been abandoned in the woods," said Evenor, the scarred man. "Who knows how long she's been running wild out here." He glanced at her dark hair in its ragged braid, the deep gray eyes. "Looks to be about twelve or so, I'd say."

"Why do you suppose she attacked us?" Goryx asked, rubbing his wrist where Atalanta had bitten him.

Phreneus shrugged. "If she hadn't jumped out, we'd never have known she was there."

Baring her teeth, Atalanta let out the loudest growl she could muster.

Evenor looked thoughtful. "It's almost as if she's try-ing to keep us from something."

"The pit!" Goryx and Phreneus said together. Goryx added, "Maybe there's something in it and she wants it for herself."

Atalanta began to thrash about and moan, anything to slow them down and give Urso more time.

Phreneus' spear jerked up. "Do you think she understands what we're saying?"

"I don't know," Evenor said. "She may have been out here so long, she's forgotten human speech. My mother told me of a child like that in her old village. The villagers tamed the child—a boy it was, small with a hump on his back—but he never learned to speak proper. Just made noises like a pig."

"I bet this one never knew how to speak in the first place," Goryx said. He put his face near Atalanta's and made grunting sounds.

Suddenly Pan's words flashed through Atalanta's mind. Dream or not, she could hear them clearly. "The lure of one's own kind is hard to resist."

Not, Atalanta thought, *if these are my kind. I can resist them forever.* She would *never* speak to them and would let them think what they liked.

She leaned forward and snarled at Goryx so loudly, he snapped his head back as if afraid of being bitten.

"I told you—Harpy's child!" he cried.

Phreneus laughed. "She has you jumping, Goryx. Leave her be. Let's check that pit."

Atalanta twisted and dragged her feet so much that in the end Evenor and Phreneus picked her up and carried her. When they reached the pit, they set her down on the ground and stared into the hole.

"Someone's rolled a log in here," Goryx said, as if the other two couldn't see for themselves.

Casting around the outside of the pit, Phreneus said, "Plenty of bear tracks."

Evenor shook his head, all the while looking at Atalanta. "But no bear." He smiled slightly. "So bear friend, have you been delaying us till the bear could climb out?"

Atalanta looked down, her lips set together in a thin, hard slash.

"What do we do now, Evenor?" Goryx asked in his unpleasant voice.

"Go after the bear," Phreneus put in.

Atalanta looked up at them and held her breath. *Please, Pan, guard my bear.* A prayer, even to a dream god, might not be amiss.

Evenor shook his head. "Who knows how far it's gotten by now. Besides"—and he smiled at Atalanta, almost as if they were conspirators—"we'll have our hands full getting the girl back to Eteos."

Goryx held up his hands. "We're not taking that Harpy's brat back with us."

"Do you think we'll be safe if we let her loose?" Evenor asked him.

Goryx looked horrified.

"And we can't very well leave her tied up," Evenor added.

"Why not?" Goryx asked.

"She's a child," Phreneus said.

"A girl child," Evenor added. Atalanta could see relief

written on his face, as if having Phreneus on his side made things easier.

"Well, it's a sorry prize we're bringing home today," Goryx said.

Evenor crouched down by her. "Listen, child, if you understand, give me a sign."

She stared at him, through him, but said nothing.

"We're going to leave your arms tied. But as long as you leave off your kicking and biting, we'll not tie your feet or gag you."

Atalanta looked down again. She'd make the walk to Eteos easy for them. Every step in that direction put more distance between Urso and these dangerous men. But nothing—nothing at all—would make her stay.

CHAPTER NINE

THE VILLAGE

hey made it to Eteos by midmorning of the next day. Atalanta had had to endure a night tied up. The men were taking no chances of her escaping.

I can wait, she thought. *I can outlast them.*

Eteos was a small huddle of three dozen mud brick-and-thatch houses around a central square in which stood a *herm,* a pillar with a stone head of Hermes at the top, for prosperity and fertility. The whole place was less than half a hectare. To Atalanta, it looked crowded and unhealthy.

The men dragged her into the square and leashed her to the pillar like an animal, then left.

I won't cry, she told herself. And indeed, she was so furious, she only glowered like a captured beast.

In the course of the afternoon, everyone in Eteos must have come out for a look. They stared at her and spoke about her as if she could not hear them or understand. The children were the worst. They seemed to make a game out of calling her names.

"Wolf girl," they cried. "Wild boar." And, "Pan's baby sister." When there were no grown-ups around, the children also hurled stones and handfuls of dirt at her just to see her snarl. Then they'd jump back, squealing and laughing, from her snapping teeth and grasping hands. For of course she couldn't reach them. A stout leather collar had been strapped around her neck and fastened shut with bronze studs. The collar was fixed to a length of thick rope that was wound around the pillar and tied with a whole string of knots that were too tight for Atalanta to work free without the help of a knife. Tethered like a wild animal, she began to act the part. At least that way she made the children keep their distance.

She knew that all she had to do to get free of the collar, the rope, the humiliations, was to talk to the people of Eteos, to let them know she was as human as they. But that would have been a defeat. For if they knew that she was one of them, that her father was dead, they would make her stay. Make her live in the village.

I can take anything, she thought, *but that.*

As the sun started down, Atalanta slumped against the post. An old woman, dressed in a frog-green garment with a bundle of kindling on her back, stopped to cluck and shake her head at the ragged captive.

"Poor child," she said through broken teeth. "Poor child."

Atalanta growled at her and the old woman left, still shaking her head.

Then two boys appeared, elbowing each other and laughing.

"Go on," said one, "go closer."

"No, she might eat me," his friend protested with a giggle.

Egging each other on, they edged toward her, smirking and chuckling.

"Hoi—wild child!" the braver one called.

Atalanta remained motionless, not even looking at them, pretending that she was half asleep.

Just let them come within reach and they'll find out how wild I really am, she thought. She'd pay them back for their taunts with broken noses and split lips. A few more feet . . .

"Get away from there!" boomed a familiar voice. "Leave the girl in peace! She's not hurting you."

At the sight of Evenor striding toward them, the boys took off, disappearing among the mud brick cottages. Atalanta opened one eye and peeked after them. Then, smelling food, she sat up.

Evenor approached her without fear, but he was careful to stay outside the measure of her rope. He set a pair of painted pottery bowls on the ground near her. One was filled with water while the other contained pieces of dried fruit, some scraps of salted meat, and a half loaf of old bread that had been softened in olive oil.

"I'll bring you some blankets to keep you warm tonight," he said, looking up at the darkening sky. "It's getting cold again. This summer seems so unpredictable. At least it shouldn't rain."

She didn't answer him. The villagers knew nothing about her. *Nothing!* Not even that she could talk.

"No one will have you in their home, you see," Evenor went on, speaking to her as if she understood him but clearly believing she did not. It was just the way she talked to Urso. "No more than they would a wolf or a wild boar. My wife is of the same mind, and I suppose I can't blame her. We've the children to consider."

He sat on his haunches and waited while Atalanta stuffed the food into her mouth by the handful. While she ate, she stared at the long scar that ran down his right arm, willing him to explain it to her.

As if he understood, Evenor pointed to the scar. "It was a boar I thought dead did this," he said. "I got too close and he'd just enough life left to pay me back for killing him. It just goes to show, you can't be too careful when you're dealing with wild things." He winked at her.

She refused to wink back. *Let him guess,* she thought. *Let him try and guess.* She would not help.

Instead, she finished her meal and pushed the bowls

away. She would eat his food to keep up her strength, but she wouldn't thank him for it.

Evenor sighed and gathered up the empty bowls. "I'll be back with the blankets, as I promised." He left, going into one of the mud-brick houses.

He kept his promise, bringing out two threadbare pieces of cloth that scarcely covered her middle. But he didn't come to see her the next day. She guessed that he'd gone off hunting. Or to work in the fields with a long, curved scythe cutting grain. She'd seen some of the men head to the fields. Atalanta was amazed to find she missed him.

A woman—probably Evenor's wife—came out of the same house and set down bowls of food and water within Atalanta's reach before hurrying away.

Some children gathered around while she ate. They started calling her names, but Atalanta bided her time. As soon as they ventured close enough, she let fly with the water bowl. She caught one boy on the side of his head, breaking the bowl in the process. He ran off howling for his mother, blood streaming down his neck.

She was glad when night came, and she could settle down under her thin blankets. This time she slipped almost immediately into a deep sleep.

Something rough and wet rubbing against her cheek woke her. Opening her eyes blearily, she saw a bulk looming dark against the quarter moon.

"Urso," she whispered.

He stopped licking her face and gave her a wide bear grin.

Rubbing her face against his neck, she made a soft growling sound, assuring him that she was all right. His answering growl was a lot deeper and louder, like the rumble of nearby thunder.

"Quiet, boy. There may be folks awake yet," she whispered to him. "How is your paw?" She pointed at it.

He held up his right foot. It seemed neither swollen nor scarred.

"Good. I'm glad of that," she told him. "Now I need help."

She showed him the rope, and he understood at once that it tethered her to the stake. Digging his claws into it, he ripped the fibers apart shred by shred. When the last few cords snapped, Atalanta jumped to her feet. She took hold of the leather collar and tried to pull it loose, but it wouldn't budge.

"Time for that later," she said.

He gave her another rumbling answer. Then, all at once, he reared up on his hind legs and sniffed the air. His head tilted, his lip curled to expose the fangs on the left side of his maw.

Atalanta knew what that meant.

Danger!

CHAPTER TEN

A SMALL HERO

Her eyes darted about, but there was no sign of any of the villagers. They were tucked into their houses, sleeping. So where was this danger?

"What is it, Urso?" she asked.

Nose down, he faced toward one of the houses.

Then she spotted what was worrying him. Even by the dim light of the quarter moon she could see the brightly colored zigzag pattern that ran down its back. Those markings were clear: The snake was venomous and deadly.

Slithering silently, it had now reached one of the cottages and slid under the ill-fitting door.

Evenor's house.

Atalanta hesitated. For all that she'd surrendered herself to the wildness of the forest, it was one of her father's teachings that still sang loud in her heart: *Help those who need help.*

She warned herself. *You have time to escape. You owe these people nothing.*

But this was Evenor's house. Of all the people of Eteos, he'd been the one to bring her blankets and food. He'd spoken kindly to her when he needn't have taken the time.

She sprinted headlong across the open ground toward the cottage, the bear only a few steps behind.

As she ran she thought: *The door is probably barred. Everyone knows to be that careful.*

Then she noticed a small window beside the door, covered only by a curtain of sackcloth and half lifted because of the softness of the night. She launched herself through the little window, brushing the frame on both sides as she tumbled in. Both her arms felt scraped raw, but nothing could stop her now.

At the thump of her landing, the two children who'd been asleep near the hearth sat bolt upright. The little girl squealed.

Atalanta lunged forward. The snake's fangs were only an inch from the child's bare foot.

"Aieeeee!" Atalanta cried as she pinned the serpent to the floor with both hands on the back of its head.

"It's the wild girl!" the boy exclaimed.

Atalanta recognized that voice. He was one of the boys who'd tormented her only the day before. But there was no time to think of that now. She had to kill the snake. And quickly.

Her father had shown her how to do this. With one hand she gripped the serpent firmly behind the head so it could not turn and bite her. At the same time, her other hand seized it by the tail. Then in a lightning swift motion, she flung the head away from her and whipped the snake through the air by its tail. Its head hit the edge of the stone hearth with a crack that split its skull and knocked a water jar onto the floor, where it shattered.

Atalanta tossed aside the dead creature and was turning to go, when she heard the sound of a curtain being yanked aside.

The hanging that separated the little cottage into two cramped rooms was pulled open, and there stood Evenor with an axe in his hand, his wife cringing behind him.

"She did it!" the boy called out.

"What?" Evenor was baffled.

"She killed the snake!" The boy's voice suddenly cracked, as if he'd just realized the danger.

"What snake?" Then Evenor spotted the dead serpent coiled on the dirt floor.

"Papa, she just flew in through the window and killed it," the little girl added. "It would've ate us."

"Blessed Artemis," her mother cried and ran over to embrace both her children. Then she put them behind her, staring at Atalanta for a long moment with a lessening fear in her eyes.

There were sudden deep-voiced cries of alarm coming from outside. Atalanta understood at once what must be happening. Turning and lifting the heavy beam that barred the door, she bolted outside.

Villagers had heard the noise—of the child's scream or the shattered jar. Coming out to investigate, they had spotted Urso. A pair of men were already advancing on him with spears.

One was Goryx, who was urging his companion, "Finish him! Finish him now!"

Standing upright, Urso slashed the air with his claws, a stance that was clearly threatening. But the men stood their ground and soon the rest of the villagers joined them, forming a semicircle of spears, pitchforks, and torches around the beleaguered bear.

Evenor had come out of the house to see what was going on, his axe still in his hand.

Turning, Atalanta seized his scarred arm.

"Please," she cried. "He won't hurt anyone. He only came to help me."

"So she talks after all," said Phreneus, rubbing his beaky nose.

Just then Urso swung a great claw and dashed aside the nearest spear point. The men moved back, well away from his reach, muttering uncertainly to one another.

Evenor lowered his axe. "Don't provoke him," he called out. "Can't you see it's the girl he's concerned about?"

"They're both equally dangerous," said Goryx. "Press on!" As if taking his own advice, he darted forward and scraped a gash across the bear's shoulder with the end of his spear.

With a roar like an avalanche, Urso lunged at him, trapping the spear beneath his paw and snapping the shaft in two with his weight.

Staggering back, Goryx squealed as if he—and not the bear—had been blooded. "Bring up the nets! Bring up the nets!"

Two men ran up, unrolling a rope net between them.

"No, stop!" Atalanta screamed, but she was too late.

The villagers flung the net over the bear. Its rope coils covered him and soon Urso flailed about, bellowing his rage, struggling to get free.

One man tried to press home too soon. His spear sailed harmlessly over the bear's hump. Urso reached out with the one paw that was not trapped and clubbed the man to the ground.

Atalanta moaned and tried to run forward, but strong hands held her, almost throwing her to the ground.

"No!" pleaded a voice. "Let her be!"

It was Evenor's wife, a long dark cloak around her nightclothes, running forward with her children right behind.

"She saved our children."

All faces turned away from the struggling bear to

look at the family with astonishment.

"It's true," Evenor confirmed in a commanding voice. "We owe her a debt. She killed a snake in our house. She's a hero, that girl."

There were some disgruntled mutterings from the men, and Phreneus called out, "A hero? Awfully small for such."

"She did. She did," called out the little girl from under her mother's sheltering arm. "Caught a serpent and killed it. With her hands! It was ready to eat me."

Her brother, braver, stood in front of his mother. He held the dead snake by the tail. "See! She could have just run off. But she saved Daphne instead."

"You heard them," said Evenor. "Let go of the girl. And let the bear alone. It'll be tame once she's loose."

The villagers were reluctant to obey, but Atalanta broke free and ran straight to Urso.

"It's all right," she told him, punctuating her words with reassuring snorts and growls. "Nobody's going to hurt you now."

"She's mad," came Goryx's voice. "That's plain enough. As soon as we've killed the bear we should dig a pit to keep her in."

CHAPTER ELEVEN

A SIGN FROM THE GODS

"Can't you see the gods have sent us a sign?" Evenor's wife demanded. "We were never meant to harm this animal or the wild girl." Her hands tightened on her children's shoulders.

Little Daphne broke from her mother's grasp and ran over to put her arms around Atalanta, which brought her close to the bear's claws.

There were mutterings in the crowd. Evenor started toward them, but his wife held him back. "Don't worry, Evenor. The bear won't harm Daphne. Can't you see— the wild girl won't let him."

"That bear broke my spear," Goryx complained. "He's nobody's tame pet."

One or two of the men grunted their agreement.

"You broke his skin first," Atalanta retorted, turning to glare at him.

Now little Daphne was astride the bear's humped neck and he turned his head slowly to look at her, though he was still bound by the net.

Evenor started forward again as the bear's tongue lolled out and gave Daphne's leg a big swipe.

"He tickles!" the child called out. "Do it again, bear." She kicked his shoulders with her bare heels, and the bear licked her a second time.

"His name," Atalanta said, "is Urso."

"Urso! Urso!" cried the little girl, putting her arms around the bear's neck.

Her father came over and lifted her off. "Poor bear. He's tired. He's had a long night and his shoulder is hurt. Come, Daphne, climb down so we can get that net off of him." He sent her off to her mother with a little push.

Reluctantly, she went back to the safety of her mother's embrace while Evenor gingerly helped Atalanta free Urso from the net.

Evenor's wife nodded her head at Atalanta. "You can stay with us," she offered. "It's much nicer inside the house than . . ." She looked with dislike at the stake in the middle of the village where the shredded rope now hung down like a dead serpent.

Shaking her matted locks, Atalanta demanded, "What about my bear?"

"We've . . . we've no room for him inside," the woman

said a bit hesitantly, adding, "but he can sleep by the door. First, though, let's see about his wound." She put her hand out. "I am Herma, Evenor's wife. You saved our children and we'll repay the debt."

Atalanta took the offered hand. "And I am Atalanta. There is no debt to repay."

By the time the rest of the villagers had returned to their own houses, Evenor had produced some oats splashed with honey for Urso. At the same time, Herma brought out a vial of ointment to spread over the gash in the bear's shoulder.

Atalanta made Urso lie down and keep still while Herma applied the salve. Herma was not a great talker, which Atalanta appreciated, and they worked side by side in companionable silence.

Once the bear was taken care of, Herma turned to Atalanta.

"I've stew in the pot. I'll bring some for you," she said almost shyly.

"That would suit me," Atalanta said. "Can I eat it out here? Urso could use the company. And . . ."

"I promise no one will hurt the bear," Evenor told her. "If it will make you easier, I'll stay outside with him."

"No, he's *my* friend," Atalanta said. "He was injured because of *me*."

Just then Herma returned with a pottery bowl brimming with stew. Atalanta took the bowl and sat down by the bear while Evenor and Herma went back into the house.

Urso coughed once, and sniffed audibly at the food until Atalanta poured half of what she'd been given in front of him. He ate it quickly, then almost immediately went to sleep.

Once she'd eaten what was left in the bowl, Atalanta lay down with her head on Urso's flank. She slept only fitfully for the rest of the night but—for the first time in weeks—with a full belly.

In the morning, Urso was gone, having sneaked away while Atalanta slept. In a way she was relieved. That way none of the villagers could change their minds about him.

The door opened and Herma came out with another bowl, this one filled with dried fruit, and bread smeared with honey. Daphne clung to her skirts.

"Where's Urso?" the little girl asked.

"Gone off by himself for a couple of days," Atalanta replied.

"But I wanted to pet him," Daphne said.

"He didn't want any more petting," her mother told her. "Now—go bring Atalanta a cup of fresh water."

Daphne hurried back into the house.

The fruit was good, but the bread was even more delicious. Almost as good—Atalanta thought—as her own mother's baking. Atalanta hadn't cared much for learning to cook and her father had been hopeless as well, so they'd gone a long time without good bread.

"With the . . . Urso . . . away, you'll be wanting some company then," said Herma.

"Company!" Atalanta exclaimed in disgust. "Why would I want that? People crowding around. Asking questions. Telling me what to do. Getting in the way. No, I don't need anybody or anything."

"That didn't stop you taking the fruit and bread and honey," Herma pointed out.

Atalanta grinned. "I said I didn't *need* it. I didn't say I didn't like it."

"Everybody needs companionship," said Herma. "You could have a good life here with us—a warm bed, a roof over your head. And I could use the help. With the baking, with the washing, with the children."

Atalanta made a face and took another bite out of the bread. "Those things belong to you, Herma, not me. I don't want them." She lowered her eyes and frowned into the bowl.

"What *do* you want?" Herma whispered the question.

"Almost everything I want has been taken from me. All I've got left is my freedom. I won't let you steal that."

"We're not trying to steal anything from you," said Herma, putting her hands out, palms up.

Atalanta's voice rose. "But you are—all these comforts, all your kindnesses. How can I stay free if you lure me that way?" Atalanta looked past the cottages to the woods beyond. That was where she belonged—not here.

Evenor suddenly appeared in the middle of their argument. He put his hands up, the sign of a peacemaker. "Maybe you can have the bread and honey *and* keep your freedom," he said.

"What do you mean?" Atalanta and Herma spoke as one.

Evenor put an arm around Herma's waist. "Well, your bear isn't around all the time, is he?"

Atalanta looked confused, but Herma clapped her hands. "Of course."

Biting her lip, Atalanta looked down at the ground. She still didn't understand.

Evenor explained. "Just as it's the bear's nature to come and go, so it could be yours. When he is away, you could live with us."

Looking up as if expecting a trap, Atalanta asked, "Why would you want that?"

Evenor smiled at her. "Fair exchange, child. We've had a hard winter, with a hard spring as well. Game is scarce, as if something's been chasing it away."

Atalanta suddenly looked down again at the ground. *Should I tell him about the beast?* Then she thought: *Since it's gone, disappeared, vanished as if it had never been, what would be the point?*

"We're having to hunt in places far from the village," Evenor continued. "And you know those parts of the forest better than we ever will."

"So . . ." Atalanta thought she knew what he was getting at.

"So if you would guide us, show us the deer trails and the watering places, show us where to set our snares, you could have a place with us here in Eteos whenever . . ."

". . . you wanted to!" Herma finished.

Putting her hands on her hips, Atalanta glared at them. "Why should I ever want to do that?"

"Child, you could get injured, it happens to the best of hunters," Evenor said.

She looked at the scar on his arm, remembered her father dying of his wounds.

"Or get sick," Herma added. "Who would take care of you then? The bear? He would make a very poor nurse."

Atalanta suddenly thought of how her father had nursed her through a bad cough the year before. And how sweet the honey on Herma's bread had tasted.

She tried to think how to answer without sounding as if she were giving in. "I'm not saying I *need* anything. But I could give you some help. In exchange for a share of the kill."

"A fair share of anything you help us catch," Evenor agreed, offering his hand.

She drew back warily. "What are you doing?"

"This is how we seal a bargain," Evenor explained. "We clasp hands."

Herma's eyes were wide. "Have you never . . . ?"

Atalanta shrugged. "It seems a funny way of doing

things, when a promise should be enough." But she suddenly recalled her father at a market fair shaking someone's hand. She held hers out and Evenor took it in his, squeezing the fingers gently.

"But remember this," Atalanta said sternly, pulling her hand back, "we're not hunting any bears."

CHAPTER TWELVE

THE HUNT

I n the month that followed, the hunters swore they'd never known such a summer for game.

"Especially after last winter and spring," said Evenor one day when they were heading home with a brace of quail and seven rabbits. Over his shoulders was slung a gutted stag. "We feared all the game was gone."

Atalanta thought briefly about the orange-tufted creature that had killed her father. Had it moved on to a fresh supply of food?

Not that she had given the creature much thought lately. Now she had a comfortable life, and on her own terms, too. As long as she could find the villagers what they needed, she had a choice spot next to a hearth on cold nights—when Urso was off on one of his solitary jaunts—and a healthy share of the meals.

Of course the littlest children, led by Daphne, shadowed her whenever she stayed over, pestering her with questions.

"Do you always sleep on the ground?"

"Do you have your meat raw, like a bear?"

"Do you and the bear ever eat people?"

Sometimes Atalanta answered. "We never ate a person yet, but if we did, we'd have to start with something small." Then she'd pounce on them making growling sounds, and they scattered like hens before a fox.

The village children her own age, though, ignored her or made faces. One or two still called her names under their breath. She guessed they were jealous, especially the girls, that she had such freedom.

Gradually, as summer blossomed and then faded under a brilliant blue sky, Atalanta found herself changing. For example, she took more care with her hair when she visited the village, combing it out and braiding it up again. At one time she'd given some thought to simply cutting it off short.

Herma had been aghast at the idea. "Only slave women have short hair."

"I'm no one's slave," Atalanta had retorted. She kept her hair long.

She'd also begun to enjoy talking with the villagers—

not just to Evenor and Herma but with many of the others—even the ones who'd shunned her before. However, one or two of them still grumbled about her presence and the influence she had on the children, a few of whom now liked to play "wild child," which mostly meant not washing and going too far into the woods on their own.

Only Goryx still complained openly.

"She'll turn on us one day," he muttered aloud. "You mark my words, she'll turn on us just like a wild beast."

One day Urso returned from marking trees around the forest to set the boundaries of his territory. He seemed reluctant to join in their usual game of gentle rough-and-tumble and didn't answer Atalanta's snorts and snuffles. Instead he growled irritably at her when she persisted.

Eventually Atalanta sat back on her haunches and fixed narrowed eyes on him.

"I know what's bothering you," she said. "I'm starting to smell of baking and wine, hearth smoke and soft covers."

Urso made a whining noise.

"It's the deal I've struck," she explained. "It's my plan. I help them out—and they leave you alone. Besides, what right do you have to grump about what I do? I don't complain when you go off by yourself, do I?"

She batted him playfully on the nose and he knocked

her onto her back with a shove of his paw. Then he rubbed his nose against her ribs until she started laughing uncontrollably.

At last he stopped and she caught her breath.

"Yes, that's right," she said. "No matter where I live, you'll still be able to sniff me out, won't you. No matter how I age. No matter if I get soft. You'll still smell the wild in me."

The next time Atalanta joined Evenor and three other hunters on a two-day trek through the forest, Urso had been gone for nearly a week.

At the end of the second day, Atalanta had helped them find a great stag, which she finished off with one well-placed arrow.

"Orion himself couldn't have tracked so surely," said Evenor. "Or flung a spear so true." He treated Atalanta like a daughter now, and she burned red and happy under his praise.

"Who's Orion?" Atalanta asked, as she knelt to gut the deer, for by rights the one who killed had to field-dress the creature. But she also got to keep the best parts.

"Why, Orion is the greatest huntsman in all Achaea," Evenor replied. "Orion-of-the-two-spears, he's called."

Phreneus added, "He's famed from far Colchis to the gardens of the Hesperides."

"What—you've never heard of Orion?" interjected Goryx. He turned to the others, a sneering disbelief on his face. "Hasn't she heard how he's killed every wild beast on the island of Chios?"

"Then I'm surprised there's any game left for the common folk," she said.

Evenor laughed and slapped his thigh.

Goryx glared at him before continuing. "There wouldn't be except every now and again Orion stops to dally with a nymph or a goddess." He nudged Phreneus. "And that gives the beasts time to multiply again."

"They say he can throw a discus as far as other men can shoot an arrow," added a hunter named Demas, a gray-haired man who rarely spoke up.

"And he's so surefooted he can walk safely across the surface of the sea," Goryx added.

Atalanta snorted through her nose. "If he tried that, he'd have drowned long ago."

Evenor laughed again.

Meaning to have the last word, Goryx said, "Orion is a true huntsman, not a hound that sniffs out prey the way you do."

Atalanta ignored him. "Have any of you ever met this wonder, this Orion?"

"No," answered Phreneus, "but everyone from Phrygia to Pylos has heard the tales."

At that, silence fell upon the little band, and they trekked back quickly to their camp. There they built up the fire and took turns with the wineskin.

Only Atalanta sat outside the circle of men, tasting

the wine but once, a soft white wine that had a touch of lavender she found refreshing. But she never took more than a taste, hating the lethargy of the next morning that came from drinking much wine. Her father had always said, "Wine is a good friend and a fierce foe."

As she sat looking into the fire, she felt a strange tingling on the back of her neck, a sure sign of some danger nearby. Without meaning to, she shivered visibly.

Seeing her uneasiness, Evenor asked, "What is it?" He had long since learned to trust her instincts.

"Ach, it's the wine," Goryx said, spitting into the fire. "Too strong for her tender belly."

Before she could put her feelings into words, a great roar shook the branches of the trees as if a gale had blown down from the north. Atalanta remembered that sound and the swallow of wine threatened to back up into her throat. She stood.

Evenor snatched up his spear, and the others followed his lead.

"What *was* that?" Goryx said.

"Hush!" Atalanta held up her hand.

Through their silence, they could hear a disturbance in the forest. An animal, a big one, was charging through the trees, breaking branches and trampling bushes as it came nearer.

"It's coming our way," said Goryx, nervously licking his lips. He set down his spear and lifted his bow instead, carefully setting the arrow in place.

"No!" Atalanta shrieked, throwing herself into Goryx's line of fire.

At that moment Urso crashed into the clearing, pulling up behind Atalanta.

"I don't know how she knows it's him," Phreneus said to the others as Atalanta stroked the mound of muscle behind Urso's neck. "Doesn't one big crash in the forest sound just like another?"

Evenor laughed, more in relief than anything else. "Not to her."

Atalanta could feel the tension in the bear's body, and as he rubbed his muzzle against her ribs, she could hear the worry in his low growl. She turned to the men. "It wasn't Urso who let out that roar."

"If it wasn't him, then what . . ." Demas began.

Looking at Atalanta's drawn face, Evenor answered, "Something a lot worse."

Urso suddenly stood on his hind feet and began sniffing the air. A menacing rumble sounded at the back of his throat.

"What is it?" Evenor asked.

"He smells something," Atalanta replied, standing. "Something he's smelled before."

The bear continued his low grumbling.

"What is it?" Evenor asked, staring up at Urso.

"I don't think he knows . . ." Atalanta whispered. But

she did. Slowly she reached for her bow and arrow and stood up even more slowly. "But Urso came here to protect me."

"Protect you from *what*?" Evenor asked.

Atalanta shook her head. "I don't know either. But I suspect it's what killed off game this winter and spring."

Suddenly close by there was a sound of foliage being trampled aside. Trees shook, shivering from the top down all around them. Another roar shattered their ears.

"That doesn't sound friendly," Demas said.

"We should make a run for it," Goryx cried, "while we still can." In the fading light of day, his face looked pale and his eyes were wide with fear.

"That would make us easy prey," said Atalanta. "And it's a long way home in the dark though the forest."

"Yes, we need to keep together so we can protect one another's backs," said Evenor.

"I don't think," Atalanta said softly, "that it's after us. I think it's after the deer." She pointed to the carcass by the fire.

"Let it have the deer then," shrilled Goryx.

"No!" Atalanta's voice was firm. "The village needs the food."

More sounds of crashing came from somewhere in the trees. Then, heedless of the humans, three rabbits and a doe trailing a fawn ran startled through the clearing, desperate to escape whatever menace was behind them.

Goryx edged away from the gutted deer, babbling. "Hide. Hide from it . . ." Then he turned and ran away from the sounds of the crashes, toward the shelter of the heaviest trees.

The others remained alert, spears in hand, but Goryx suddenly screamed, and they all spun around. All they could see were the bottoms of his sandals vanishing into the undergrowth as if he'd been snatched away by a giant hand. Then there was a wild thrashing in the treetops and finally a sickening sound of bone snapping.

"What is it?" whispered Evenor. "Have you seen this thing before?"

"No. Not entirely. Some of it. Its back. And its paw. Its *huge* paw. Whatever the creature is, it killed my father," she said quietly. But there was no quiet in her belly. Her mouth was filled with the salt tang of anger and fear. She had her bow out, an arrow in place.

The three men and Atalanta edged forward to the spot where Goryx had disappeared. They rammed their spears into the greenery, trying to flush out the beast. But whatever had been there was already gone. Above them, branches on the trees suddenly started shaking as if in the middle of a storm.

Urso's growl was as constant as summer thunder.

"Quiet, boy," Atalanta said, her arm starting to tremble with the pull of the bow.

"I see him!" Demas shouted, and the three men plunged into the undergrowth.

Atalanta stayed back, tense and alert.

No sooner had her companions gone than a shape erupted into the clearing on the other side, something orange like a mountain cat, but much *much* larger. Atalanta turned the moment she heard it. The beast was bull high at the shoulder, with long upper fangs over-hanging its lower lip, ears tufted in orange and gold, a shaggy mane, serpent's tail, a large scar across one of its front paws, and a charnel house smell. And it had . . .

"Wings," Atalanta cried. "I should have guessed it before now. Wings!"

Urso reared up and roared, part challenge, part fear.

The beast didn't bother to answer. Instead it took one leap toward them and glared at Atalanta who faced it with her drawn bow.

There was a long pause as girl and beast stared at each other. Then the creature shook its shaggy head and backed away. Turning, it pounced on the gutted deer, and with a mighty sweep of its golden wings rose into the air with the carcass in its claws, and was gone.

CHAPTER THIRTEEN

VICTIMS OF THE BEAST

talanta's father had always said: "Trust what you see, hear and smell, just the way the beasts of the wild do. Don't let your mind conjure fancies out of your fears."

But now her mind told her such a thing as the winged lion could not exist. Yet her senses—what she'd seen, heard, and smelled—told her the creature was real. For a moment she was stunned into immobility, as if she'd been encased in a block of ice.

Sensing her confusion, Urso leaned comfortingly against her, almost pushing her over. It was only then that Atalanta found she could move again.

Evenor burst back out of the greenery, bow and arrow at the ready, and saw how shaken she looked.

"Atalanta, are you all right?"

"I *saw* it," Atalanta said, scarcely breathing. She pointed at the empty space by the fire. "I saw the creature. It took the stag, picked the carcass up as if the thing weighed no more than a piece of straw."

"What kind of beast was it?" Evenor asked, casting about for some sign of the creature's trail.

"It was bigger than a bull," she said slowly, "like a mountain cat but enormous. With claws, a mane, a scaly serpent's tail . . . wings." Her voice died away. She knew the description sounded absurd.

"Where did it go?" Evenor asked with an uneasy frown.

"It flew off," said Atalanta. "That way." She gestured to a spot above the trees.

At that moment Phreneus and Demas appeared, supporting Goryx between them.

Goryx was bruised and scratched and blood trailed from a wide row of tooth marks on his left leg. His eyes were glazed with shock and his lips twitched as though he were muttering wordlessly to himself. But—miraculously—he was alive.

The two hunters laid their stricken companion down by the campfire and did their best to dress his wounds, pouring water and wine into the bloody punctures.

"Did anyone see the thing that did this?" Phreneus asked. "I can't believe the size of that bite."

"I saw it," said Atalanta. She repeated the description she'd given Evenor.

Demas shook his head. "Girl's lost her wits," he grumbled. "Must have been a mountain cat gave her a scare."

"There's nothing wrong with *my* wits," Atalanta told him hotly. "I've seen mountain cats before. *And* killed them. This was no cat. Ask Goryx. He must have seen it."

"I don't think he saw anything," said Phreneus, looking down at the wounded man. "I think his own fright is all he remembers."

Goryx was twitching fitfully where he lay, which was making it difficult for Demas to wind a bandage around his injured leg.

"For all we know, that beast's on its way to the village," Evenor said grimly. "We have to get back and warn everyone."

"In the dark?" Demas objected.

"We have to go. For the village's sake. And to get a healer for Goryx," Phreneus pointed out.

At the sound of his name, Goryx groaned.

"We can make torches to light our way," said Atalanta. "Wild creatures are afraid of fire."

Evenor agreed. "Atalanta, you know this forest better than I know the faces of my children. You can guide us back, can't you—even in the dark?"

Atalanta nodded.

"Right then, let's get Goryx up," Evenor said decisively.

They helped him to his feet and handed him his spear.

Then Evenor leaned close to Goryx and addressed him urgently. "Can you walk, man?" When there was no reaction he repeated the question. "Goryx, can you walk?"

For a minute, Goryx's clouded eyes cleared. Then he nodded. Gingerly he tested his wounded leg and then, leaning heavily on his spear, he hobbled forward a few paces. "Yes, I can walk. I wish I could run."

Quickly, the men made four torches out of long branches and twig heads, wound about with pieces of their shirts. They held the torches into the campfire till one by one, they blazed.

Atalanta took the lead with Urso by her side, his ears standing up alertly. The nimbus of torchlight stretched only a few feet ahead, and with the light came accompanying shadows. Atalanta knew she'd have to rely on the bear's instincts to alert them to any presence of the beast.

Evenor followed close behind, and at his back came Demas, one hand under Goryx's arm. Phreneus was their nervous rear guard, flinching at every rustle in the undergrowth and jabbing his spear at irregular intervals as if to keep a whole host of imaginary enemies at bay.

It was dawn when Eteos finally came in sight, and only then did Atalanta relax a little.

With a great loud whuffle, Urso abandoned them at the edge of the village, bounding back into the forest.

Atalanta turned for a moment, watching him go. She wished she could follow. To keep him safe. But right now she knew the villagers needed reassurance.

And reinforcements, she thought.

As they drew nearer to the cluster of cottages, she saw that the whole place was already astir, like a disturbed beehive.

On the far side of the village, across the square and to the right, a buzzing crowd had gathered around the goat pen. The hunters headed straight there, and when the crowd parted to let them through, Atalanta saw that five of the goats in the pen had been slaughtered, their throats and bellies ripped open and two of them partially eaten. The soft parts.

"It's been here already," Phreneus said, shaking his head.

"Yes," Evenor agreed. "Nothing else could have done this much damage."

Goryx began to tremble uncontrollably again. Atalanta could hear his teeth chattering. She put her hand out to him, but he shook her off, almost angrily.

Finding his wife, Herma, in the crowd, Evenor said, "Take Goryx to his cottage and have someone tend his wounds before his leg swells up."

"What happened to him?" Herma asked, eyeing the bloody bandage.

"Nearly the same thing that happened to these goats," Atalanta said.

For a long moment after that there was silence. Finally one man asked the hunters, "What manner of creature is it that can move so fast and strike so brutally in the dark? Not even a mountain cat or a bear does this much damage."

"Atalanta saw it," Evenor said.

"What did it look like, girl?" someone else called out.

"I only saw it for a second," Atalanta replied, "but it was a monster. High as a bull at the shoulder, in the likeness of a cat, but with wings."

A skeptical murmur passed through the crowd.

"Does it have a name?" someone else cried. "This monster?"

"I've never seen another like it," Atalanta replied.

"Whatever this creature is," said Phreneus, "we must warn the other villages that they need to guard their animals—and themselves."

"I'll go," said Evenor, "and Atalanta should come with me. To describe it properly."

Atalanta trembled, with fear as well as fatigue, but she gave her silent agreement to Evenor's plan.

Only Herma seemed to notice her shaking.

"Not until you've had a proper meal and some sleep," she told them firmly, before dragging Goryx off to be tended.

CHAPTER FOURTEEN

LAND OF DANGER

A talanta found it easier to eat than to sleep. Her dreams exhausted her more than the long night's trek through the forest, dreams of teeth dripping blood, dreams of wings of flame.

It was a relief when Evenor shook her awake.

"There are a few hours of daylight left," he said. "If we leave now, we can reach the next village before dark."

"Can we wait for Urso?" Atalanta asked, suddenly missing her furry friend.

"He'll have to find us on his own," Evenor told her. "There's little time to lose."

Phreneus insisted on coming with them. Since he still seemed shaken by the beast's attack, Atalanta was surprised that he wanted to be part of a journey that could prove so dangerous. Then she realized that it would be worse for him to remain behind, haunted by what had happened to them in the night forest. By coming with them, at least he had a chance to face his fears.

They reached the next village, Phylos, that evening, a place smaller and far dirtier than Eteos. There they learned that a hunting party had already lost two of its dogs to some wild creature, and they'd been unable to find any of the remains.

"Completely gone in an instant," one of the men explained. "They were tracking well ahead of us, baying on the trail. Then we heard a strange yelp from one of them. From the other, only silence. But by the time we got to where their footprints ended—they were gone."

"*Clean* gone," added another man.

"We know the creature that did this," Atalanta said.

The head huntsman stared at her for a moment with disdain, his nose wrinkling as if he smelled something bad. He was a tall, lean man, with lines as deep as craters across his brow. Turning away from Atalanta to Evenor, he said, "If you think this creature of yours is responsible, then what is it exactly?"

"Not ours . . ." Atalanta began, but Evenor put a hand on her arm to silence her.

"We only had a glimpse of it," he told the tall huntsman. "All I can tell you is that it's big. Very big. Body of a great lion but with wings. Moves as fast as a bird. Guard your herd animals. Take them into the houses at night. Travel only in the daylight or in large parties that can defend themselves."

"For Hermes' sake, don't go after it alone," Phreneus added.

Atalanta didn't say anything more. It was clear that the hunters wouldn't value the same information from a girl.

They heard a similar story in every farm and village they came to: cattle and sheep killed in the fields, goats and pigs carried off by an unseen predator, hunters coming upon their prey already slaughtered and stripped to the bone.

"This beast is unstoppable," Phreneus said.

"*No* beast is unstoppable," Atalanta said. "Or so my father used to say."

"Your father," Phreneus pointed out, "died under this one's claws."

Evenor gave him a look that shut him up. "This beast," Evenor mused, "is eating for more than one."

For a moment all three of them were silent thinking about the implications of that.

"It's a female?" Atalanta said at last. She tried to remember what she'd glimpsed of it: head, mouth, haunch, wings, tail. She tried to put the entire picture together in her mind and see it as female. She failed. It had seemed overwhelmingly male: fierce, bloody, frightening.

"A female?" she asked again, her uncertainty clear in those two words.

"Or a male bringing back food to its mate," Evenor said.

The thought that there were two of the creatures—and maybe more—made them all shudder, and sweat suddenly sprang up on either side of Phreneus' beaked nose.

At last they came to the largest village in the region, Mylonas, where the great fairs were held and where people from all the surrounding villages gathered to trade with one another.

Atalanta had been twice to Mylonas with her father and had hated every minute of it.

There were no fairs or festivities going on now. Instead the same air of fear that they'd met in other villages hung over the houses.

They were welcomed by the headman, Labrius, an old friend of Evenor's. He was gray haired, and looked to be about sixty, but still had the lean strength of one who'd spent his life laboring in the fields from dawn till dusk.

"We've come about a strange beast that's been terrorizing the villages around here," Evenor began.

"Come, come, my friends," said Labrius. "I make it a policy never to discuss difficult business on an empty stomach." He led them to his cottage, a large stone house with four rooms in a semicircle around an open courtyard.

Evenor, Atalanta, and Phreneus joined him and his two sons at a table in the courtyard, where his wife served them with a sweet red wine poured from a large jar called a krater, and bowls filled with fresh stewed vegetables.

Atalanta didn't wait for an invitation, but straightaway started on her food.

The men laughed at her, but they began to eat as well. Labrius waited until they were almost done before allowing anyone to speak.

Finally he leaned back in his chair, wiping his mouth with the back of his hand. "So, my friend Evenor, what makes you leave your wife and children to come here?"

Evenor began telling him the story of their hunt, of the death of Atalanta's father, the maiming of Goryx, and all of the tales of carnage in the villages and farms between Eteos and Mylonas. He was careful to praise Atalanta, her skills, her heroics.

Occasionally Phreneus interrupted to add more to the story, usually elaborating on the bloodier parts.

Having learned her lesson in Phylos, Atalanta didn't interrupt but instead had a second helping of the stew.

Labrius listened intently, nodding more than once to show that he understood. When Evenor finished, Labrius leaned forward in his chair.

"We, too, have lately had our share of misfortunes," he said. "Hardly any deer or boar this winter, then a sudden surplus of them. And now—goats and cattle taken.

But the worst came two nights ago. Echthenes heard his cows bellowing with fear. 'A bear,' he told his wife, before running out with his spear to protect them. He was a good huntsman, Echthenes. The best." Labrius' eyes were suddenly moist, but he didn't cry. "We found his mangled body in the midst of six dead cows, the broken spear by his side. The cows were all partially eaten, but he wasn't, which was a small blessing. At least we could bury him. The bite marks on his back and spear arm were enormous, much too deep and wide spaced for a bear."

For a moment there was silence at the table, then one of Labrius' sons—a stoop-shouldered man of thirty, spoke. "Passing travelers have told us the same stories from all over Arcadia. Whatever this monster is, it's spreading terror throughout the whole kingdom."

The other son, handsome where his brother was plain, added, "It's said King Iasus is assembling a party to hunt the beast down."

"Who's King Iasus?" Atalanta whispered to Phreneus, who was sitting on her right.

"King of Arcadia," Phreneus whispered back. "Though I for one have never seen him."

What's the use in having a king if you never see him? Atalanta thought, though she didn't say it aloud. Instead she reached for some black-skinned olives.

"This is a curse sent by the gods," Labrius' stern-faced wife declared loudly. She thumped a jug onto the table to emphasize her point.

A long silence greeted her.

At last Atalanta spoke. "What have the gods to do with it?"

The old woman scowled down at her. "Think, girl, think. When a crime has gone unpunished by men, the gods will send a punishment of their own."

"Now, now, Iole," Labrius cautioned her, "we'll have no talk of crimes and punishment here."

Iole snorted and placed her hands on her hips. "What do you know, old man? You sit all day with your cronies and drink wine and it muddles what few wits you have left. Perhaps someone unknown to us has insulted the gods . . ." Before she could go on, there was a shrill uproar from the center of the village.

Atalanta could make out cries of panic. "Run!" she heard. "Run or you'll die!"

She grabbed up her bow, and Evenor and Phreneus took up their spears. Then the three of them ran toward the sound of the cries, Labrius and his sons right after them.

"Is it the beast?" Atalanta shouted as they ran.

"In the village center? In daylight?" Evenor replied. "Surely not."

But Atlanta thought, *I have seen the creature. It would dare anything.*

They pulled aside to avoid the fleeing people. Behind the runners a cloud of dust billowed up and from it came a ferocious bellowing.

"That's not the monster," Atalanta said, turning to Evenor. "He roars."

"Roar, bellow—it's all the same," said Labrius, having caught up with them.

"Papa, you're too old . . ." said the stoop-shouldered son.

"Get back," his other son said at the same time.

Just then the cause of the commotion came into view. It was a bull, kicking and snorting and tossing its head from side to side, its sharp horns hooking through the air. It was in a murderous fury. Behind it one man already lay dead, two others cringed, wounded, against a wall. Broken pots, ripped baskets, and a table with its legs broken, lay in the bull's path.

"That's Gallo's best bull," Labrius said. "It must have broken free of its enclosure."

Atalanta stared at the crazed beast. "It looks in pain."

The bull lunged at one of the wounded men, who managed to crawl around the overturned table. Losing sight of its prey, the beast turned away and charged to the other side of the square, snorting. It stamped its hooves against the stones of the village well, knocking half of it into rubble.

Licking her lips, Atalanta took an arrow from her quiver and set it into her bow. *Where is a vital spot?* she wondered, knowing that just wounding the bull would only madden it further.

"Hold a minute," said Evenor, who clearly had had the same thought.

Atalanta lowered the bow.

Labrius cried out, "But we have to save them or there'll be more dead this day."

Hearing their voices, the bull lifted its great head, its small eyes reddened with pain. It pawed the ground three times, then lowered its head and started toward them.

Atalanta lifted the bow again, thinking that they no longer had a choice. She pulled back on the bowstring and was just sighting on the beast's eye, when a huge hand pushed her gently aside.

"Be careful, girl," came a rich, confident voice. "That's a mighty big bow you have there. Better leave this to me."

CHAPTER FIFTEEN

THE CHALLENGE

T he speaker strode past Atalanta and Evenor, tossing a pair of lances and a heavy pack to the ground. He was the biggest man Atalanta had ever seen, a full head and shoulders taller than Evenor. His long black hair was tied back in a knot and his black beard was cropped short. He wore a deerskin tunic that must have taken the hides of three stags, and a lion skin cloak draped over his shoulders. His muscles bunched alarmingly.

The bull sighted this new threat, bellowed again, and charged.

The newcomer stood his ground. Weaponless, he fell into a fighting crouch, arms outstretched. "Come, bull," he said, pounding his right fist to his chest, "I dedicate your death to the people of this village."

Atalanta gasped in horror. *Surely the fool will be trampled to death,* she thought. *He may be big, but the bull is bigger.*

The sound of the bull's hooves thudding on the ground was louder than thunder, but the man did not flinch. At the last instant he seized the bull by its horns and twisted its neck violently to one side. The beast's hooves kicked at him, but he forced the animal back, driving his hip into its flank and toppling it to the ground. Falling on top of the bull, the man flexed his bulging muscles and gave the horns a mighty wrench. The bull's neck broke with an awful crack.

For a moment everything was silent. Then the villagers burst from hiding, waving their arms and cheering.

"Who *is* that?" Atalanta asked as people rushed by her to surround the giant and shake his hand.

"By the gods, girl," Labrius said, grinning, "there is only one man it could be. The height, the fearlessness, the lion skin." He pushed aside the villagers to welcome the giant to Mylonas.

"It's Orion," Evenor said.

"I thought he was just a story," Atalanta said.

Phreneus rubbed a finger along the side of his nose. "What a story then. An epic!" He laughed out loud.

Evenor laughed with him. "Epic he may be. But he's

our salvation for sure." He signaled Atalanta and Phreneus to join the villagers, and they pushed their way into the crowd.

"See here," Orion was saying, lifting up the dead bull's flank. "It's been stung. Scorpion's my guess. The pain of that sting would drive any creature wild before the poison kills it."

The crowd gazed down at the mark on the bull's flank, but Atalanta gaped at the man. *He looks like a god,* she thought. Then remembering Pan, added, *Or how a god should look.*

"Whatever it was that drove it to destruction makes no difference now," Labrius said in a voice pitched so that everyone could hear. "We will feast well tonight, my friends." He turned to the crowd and spread his arms wide. "A feast to celebrate the strength and courage of our guest, Orion—the greatest hunter in all the world!"

A huge cheer went up, and Atalanta found herself cheering as well.

The feast was held that night in the village square, on the very spot where the bull had been stopped. Kraters of wine and platters of roast meat were passed around. The women of Mylonas had baked fresh bread and there were pots of boiled onions and beans. Little honey cakes were served at the meal's end, when the storytellers— dark-haired twins from Salonika—told the tale of Orion and the Maddened Bull, a story which only grew in its telling.

"I said it would be an epic." Phreneus' nose was bright red with all the drinking, and he laughed too loudly, snorting as he did so.

Atalanta cringed at the sound. She was seated between Evenor and Phreneus. Along with Labrius and the other village leaders, they shared a table with Orion. Atalanta had been included because Evenor had insisted. Otherwise she would have been relegated to serving the food and wine, with the other young women.

Behind them, all around the table, stood the rest of the villagers, lips smeared with greasy meat. They all seemed drunk, not so much on wine as on Orion's presence.

The hero's two great hunting spears lay on the ground at his side. Each of them was longer than he was tall, and capped with a gleaming bronze point.

Orion's voice boomed out over the crowd, yet he didn't seem to be straining to be heard. "A messenger from your king Iasus reached me in Elis, to the north," he explained between draughts of wine. "A savage beast, 'twas said, is ravaging your fair land. The king offered me any reward I asked for if I would come to Arcadia and kill it."

This news traveled a second time through the crowd, as if repeating it made it even more true.

Labrius beamed and lifted his cup. "May the gods

praise Iasus for bringing you here."

All through the crowd cups were lifted.

Labrius added, "We are mostly farmers here, Orion. We haven't the skill to hunt down this monstrous creature on our own."

Grinning, Orion put down his cup and leaned forward, elbows on the table. "So what *is* this creature? Bear? Rabid wolf? An old lion taking placid cows and toddlers who have wandered off down the path?"

Labrius put his cup down as well and spread his hands helplessly. "We don't know. All we know is that it kills without mercy."

Orion laughed, throwing his head back. Then he looked at Labrius. "All beasts kill without mercy," he said. "Mercy is a human failing. Never think of an animal as you would a person, otherwise you'll misjudge it and make an error that could cost you your life." He picked up a steak bone and began gnawing on it.

The others nodded as if this were the greatest wisdom. But Atalanta had heard something like it before, from her father.

"Atalanta has seen it," piped up Phreneus, putting his hand on her head, as if by touching her he shared in her feat. "The girl," he added unnecessarily.

Orion set down the bone and stared at her.

"She says—" Phreneus continued before Orion silenced him with a raised hand.

"Unless she's lost her tongue to this beast, she can

speak her own words better than you can," he said. He kept his eyes fixed on her, his gaze mesmerizing.

Atalanta took a moment before saying anything. She wanted it clear that she was speaking hunter to hunter, not as a bidden child. At last she said, "It was very quick. I saw only a mane, claws, fangs hanging down thus"— she made her fingers into teeth—"serpent's tail." She took a big breath. "And a pair of wings."

"Were the wings feathered?"

She stared blankly at him.

"Were they the wings of a bird," Orion prompted her, "or those of a bat or an insect?"

Atalanta nodded. No one had thought to ask such a thing before. She closed her eyes for a moment and saw the beast again. Opening her eyes she said, "Bird wings. Feathered. Set high on the shoulders."

There was silence in the inner circle and—except for a child crying beyond the nimbus of the central fire— the crowd was silent, too.

Orion continued to stare at Atalanta for a moment more, stroking his chin as if in thought. Then he picked up the steak bone again. "She sees true," he said, gesturing with the bone. "Like the hawk and the wolf. I *like* that."

Atalanta blushed under his praise.

"Then what manner of creature is it?" Labrius asked, almost in a whisper.

Atalanta and the others leaned forward to hear Orion's answer.

"What manner of creature?" He leaned back casually. "It wasn't spawned in Arcadia, though you have your share of strange animals here. *If* you know where to look for them." He grinned, as if to say he alone knew such things.

"Then where . . ." Atalanta asked, trying to hurry him along.

But he would not be hurried. Storytelling, it seemed, was part of his greatness and the folk of Mylonas drank it in.

"From Sparta?" called out someone from the crowd.

"The Long Island?" cried another.

"The land of the Keshites?" asked a third.

It had become a guessing game and Orion let it go on for some time. Then, suddenly bored, he waved his hand to cut them off.

"No," he said, "from the girl's description, I'd say this creature is kin to the sphinx, the chimera, and the manticore. If it's what I think it is, it dwells in the scorching deserts of the East where it's called a *layish*, or in our tongue, a mantiger." He pronounced it with a drawl: *man'-ta-jur*.

Evenor leaned forward over the table as if to challenge Orion. "If it lives so far away, what is it doing here?"

Orion narrowed his eyes but didn't otherwise show he felt challenged at all. "Perhaps drought has driven it out, or it's a young male without its own territory. Or . . ." He looked carefully around the table, including those who stood as well as those who sat, then said in a hushed voice, "Perhaps it has been lured here."

"Lured?" Labrius asked. "By whom?"

But Atlanta had already guessed. "By the gods," she whispered.

Orion heard her. "Always a possibility," he said. "But whatever has brought the mantiger to Arcadia, it will soon be sorry it has crossed paths with *Orion*." He slapped himself on the chest, a blow that would have broken the bones of any other man.

The crowd laughed and roared its approval.

Atalanta stirred uneasily in her chair. She was not certain what to make of Orion. He was big, yes, and certainly brave. Everyone said what a fine hunter he was. But she was uncomfortable when he began to boast. Her father had always said, "Do not praise yourself while there are others around who can sing your praises for you." She bit her lip, then asked, "Are you going to hunt by yourself, then?"

He smiled at her condescendingly. "A beast that roams this far and wide and seems to have no fixed lair? I may be a hero, but I'm no fool, girl. It will take a hunting party to encircle it, to pen it in."

Encircle a flying beast? she thought, but didn't say it aloud.

"Of course," Orion continued, "I'll want the best hunters I can find to accompany me."

"I'll come," Evenor volunteered.

Orion eyed Evenor shrewdly, taking in his lean frame, his sharp, intelligent face, and the scar that ran the length of his arm. "A boar," he said, recognizing at once the nature of the wound. "Took it for dead, did you?"

Evenor nodded.

"How many boar have you killed since?"

"Seven," Evenor replied.

Orion looked away from him and spoke to the crowd. "A man who's never taken a wound is too cautious to be of any use to me. A man who fears to close for the kill because of his wound is likewise of no use." He turned back to Evenor and nodded approvingly. "You'll do."

"What about Herma and the children?" Phreneus objected.

"You tell them, my friend. They'll understand," said Evenor. "Until this beast is killed, none of us will be safe. I must do my part, for everyone's sake."

"I'm coming, too," said Atalanta flatly.

Orion raised an amused eyebrow. "This is man's work."

Atalanta stood. "What does being a man have to do with finding and killing the beast? I'm the only one who's seen it and lived to tell the tale."

"So you are," Orion agreed. "Therefore you shouldn't tempt the Fates a second time."

"I thought you said a hunter made cautious by his wound was of no use to you. I haven't been made cautious," she said quickly.

"You weren't wounded," he pointed out, then smiled. A titter ran around the crowd.

"That beast killed my father," Atalanta replied hotly. "And that's a wound deeper than one to my own flesh. Besides, there's no better tracker in these woods than me." She thought briefly: *Now I'm boasting as much as Orion.*

"She's right," Evenor conceded. "She's the best I've ever known." Turning to Atalanta, he asked urgently, "Are you sure you want to do this?"

"It doesn't matter what *she* wants," Orion cut him off curtly. "This hunt is mine."

"I thought it was the king's hunt," Atalanta said.

"Mind your tongue, girl," Labrius warned her.

Atalanta was about to snap back at him, but Evenor shook his head, effectively silencing her. He turned to address Orion. "No one knows the forest or the ways of the local animals like Atalanta. She would be a great help to the hunt."

"I can see there's something of the wild about her," said Orion, smiling again to take the sting from his words. "But she'll simply slow us down. In this hunt, speed is of the essence."

"Give me a chance and I'll win a place in your hunt," said Atalanta.

"Win it? How?" He seemed amused.

Without thinking, she blurted out, "By . . . by defeating you in a footrace."

Orion let out a huge laugh that was soon taken up by the others, all except Evenor.

Atalanta waited for the noise to subside. "I hear you're so fast you can run over the surface of the sea," she said. "So if I beat you, will you let me join your hunt?"

"Girl, you could no more beat me than you could outrun the wind," Orion said mockingly.

"I can run as fast as a bear," Atalanta answered him. It was no boast, but the simple truth.

Orion took a thoughtful sip from his wine cup. All eyes were on him now. Would he accept the challenge or dismiss it? Atalanta was gambling that he couldn't afford to lose face in front of all these men.

"Very well," Orion agreed at last. "We'll race in the morning."

Atlanta grinned and raised her own wine cup, but she didn't drink further. She would need a clear head as well as strong legs to win that race.

CHAPTER SIXTEEN

TWO NATURES

O rion entertained the company late into the night with tales of his adventures, but Atalanta quickly heard enough about his strength, courage, and cleverness, all delivered in a lazy drawl. She stood and glanced about.

Labrius called her over. "One of our people can find you a pallet in his cottage for the night," he offered. Then with a twinkle, he added, "You'll need a good night's rest if you're to beat Orion tomorrow."

Everyone at the table laughed loudly at the joke.

"She'll need a hundred nights' rest to do that!" his handsome son called, and the laughter redoubled.

"I don't need a roof over my head," Atalanta said sharply. "I'll sleep under the stars."

"Surely not," said Labrius. "What about the mantiger?"

"I'll shelter high in a tree," she replied. "The thing may have wings, but it's too heavy to roost." What she didn't say was that she hoped that Urso had found her trail. But if he had, she knew he'd never come openly into a place like Mylonas.

Snatching up her bow, arrows, and spear, she stomped off into the nearby woods. There she found an oak high enough to keep her from the ground animals but with a canopy deep enough to discourage the mantiger's attention should it still be close.

Climbing the tree easily, she settled down in a crotch, making certain that her quiver of arrows was slung on a branch within easy reach, and that both bow and spear were at hand. But it was hard getting to sleep with so much loud singing and laughing going on back at the village. The people of Mylonas were celebrating as heartily as if Orion had already slain the beast and taken its hide as a trophy. But at last she drifted off, only to be awakened by a soft whistle.

At first she thought it must be a breeze blowing through the trees. Then she realized the air was still; what she heard was a pipe tune.

Tucking her knife into her belt, and taking her spear in hand, she shimmied down the tree, following the sound.

Suddenly a familiar musk invaded her nostrils.

"Urso," she called as her feet touched the ground. She turned, and in the dim light of the shrouded moon, she saw him.

He wasn't alone. Curled up on the ground under an ash tree, he had rested his head in the lap of a figure she recognized. For a moment jealousy pierced her like a poisoned dart.

When he saw Atalanta, Pan lowered the pipes. "Ah, the little huntress," he said in that low, musical voice. "I wondered when you'd show up."

"You again!"

"You could at least try to sound pleased to see me," Pan said. "Why, the nymphs and shepherds throughout Arcadia rejoice at the very sight of me."

"Well, I am neither nymph nor shepherd, and I can do without the sight of you," Atalanta said.

Pan smiled. He didn't have good teeth. "Is that so?" He scratched Urso behind the ear and the bear made a deep-throated noise that was almost a purr. "You can do without me but obviously not without your fellow humans. I said that would happen, remember? *The lure of one's own kind is hard to resist.* Are you enjoying their company?"

"Enjoying isn't the word I would use," Atalanta said. "But at least we are all after the same thing—the beast that slew my father." She set the butt of the spear into the ground and leaned on it.

"Very high-minded I'm sure," said Pan. He patted the

top of the bear's head. "But what do you think that great bully Orion would do if he found Urso here?"

"I'll see to it he doesn't find Urso," Atalanta said. Then watching the bear rub his muzzle up against Pan's cheek, she said softly, "Urso seems very comfortable with you."

"We're old friends. Do you object?"

"He can do what he likes," Atalanta declared with a shrug, though she knew she did care, desperately. "He doesn't need my permission." She suddenly found herself irked with the forest god. "Or yours."

"It's not a matter of permission," said Pan. "It's a matter of nature. You have been fighting human nature trying to live like a beast in the forest. Now Urso is fighting his animal nature in order to be close to you. His very blood tells him to return to the deep forest to begin the cycle of life afresh. But he also knows that you need him, that without his help you may die on this hunt."

Urso got up and padded over to Atalanta, nuzzling her with his big wet nose.

Pan stood as well. On his bowed goat's legs he was the same size as Orion, towering over her.

Atalanta looked up at him. Suddenly something became clear to her. "You *know* this beast, this mantiger, don't you?"

The woodland god wrinkled his long nose and stuck out his tongue in distaste. "That creature doesn't belong in my Arcadia. It carries the stink of the eastern deserts. If you can rid the woodlands of it, you'll have my blessings."

"So it *is* from far away," Atalanta mused aloud.

Pan nodded.

"Is it possible the gods brought it here then?"

Pan spat to one side, and where it landed a yellow flower popped up. "If it's oracles you want, go to that boaster Apollo. Or if it's wisdom you're looking for, badger that know-it-all-tell-it-ever Athena. I'm only here for good times and fun."

Atalanta was surprised at his anger toward his fellow gods. But she thought it best not to mention that. Instead she said, "You seem to know a lot about what Urso needs."

"Of course. That's because we are brothers."

"You're not a bear," Atalanta pointed out. "And I was the one raised in the same litter with him."

"Nevertheless, this is the last journey he can make with you," Pan said. His face was suddenly sad, pulled down like a beeswax candle melted in the heat.

"But we'll still see each other, won't we?" asked Atalanta. "He'll still come to visit me?" She clutched the spear so hard it made a print in her palm.

"No, child," said Pan gravely. "After this hunt, the cords of Fate that bind you together will be severed forever. He must go and start a family of his own, while you must find the family that you lost."

His words made the hairs on the back of Atalanta's neck stand up. She looked left, then right, as if a predator were nearing.

"What do you mean?" she asked, her mouth suddenly dry. "What family?"

By way of reply, Pan lifted the reed pipe back to his mouth and blew a long, low note that washed over her like a soft mist. It muddled her mind and she felt herself sinking to the ground, eyes closing.

When she opened them again, she was back in the tree and Urso was stretching up and licking her leg.

She sat up stiffly. Pan was gone. *If,* she thought, *he'd ever been there at all.* Suddenly she was sure the entire conversation had been no more than a dream.

Scratching the top of Urso's head, she whispered, "Good night, brother-bear. Thank you for standing guard." Then she curled into the crotch of the tree and slept once more.

CHAPTER SEVENTEEN

THE RACE

I t was an hour past dawn when Atalanta woke. Her body was stiff and there was a terrible taste in her mouth. Climbing down from the tree, she found Urso had already left.

Better that way, she thought, *with the Mighty Hunter so near.* She brushed away the bear tracks with her foot.

Going back to the village, she located the well, and hauled up a bucket of water, which she splashed liberally over her. Then she stretched her legs, first one and then the other, to ensure that her muscles didn't cramp in the middle of the race.

It wasn't long before people began emerging from their houses. In spite of their long celebratory evening, no one wanted to miss the fun.

They're here, Atalanta thought, *to cheer Orion on.*

As if answering his name, Orion suddenly came out of the door of Labrius' house, stretching his arms and yawning. Even this unheroic display was enough to prompt a loud round of applause. He filled the bucket from the well and drained it in one long draught.

Just then Phreneus emerged from one of the humbler cottages. Looking from the tall huntsman to Atalanta, he shook his head.

I suppose, Atalanta thought, *he means I might as well go home now.*

Evenor appeared at last with Labrius. Spying Atalanta, he hurried over. In a low voice no one else could hear, he said, "A prayer to swift-footed Hermes might be a good idea, Atalanta."

"Why? Because you think I can't win without the gods' help?" She felt cross. "Isn't that just the same as cheating?"

"Not if they're helping Orion as well."

"Well, they would, wouldn't they," she said.

Evenor couldn't help it. He began to laugh.

"Why are you laughing?"

"I am reminded of a race run in our village many years ago. A man named Charmus ran for three miles with five others, and he came in seventh." He chuckled as he spoke.

She looked puzzled. "How seven?"

"A friend of his went along crying, 'Keep it up,

Charmus!' and arrived ahead of him. If he'd five more friends, he would have come in twelfth!" He began laughing again.

It took Atalanta a moment to get the joke, and when she did, she began to laugh, too. Soon they were howling together, till tears ran from their eyes.

When the laughter passed at last, Atalanta handed Evenor her bow, spear, quiver, and belt. Then she took the leather thong from around her neck with the boar's head ring.

"Will you . . ." she began.

"Of course." He gathered them to his chest. "As if they were my own."

Atalanta looked over to where Orion was stripping down to his loincloth and sandals, leaving himself as unencumbered as possible. Seeing his swelling muscles and powerful legs, she wondered for the first time if she had simply made a fool of herself by challenging him. Yes, she'd chased Urso through the forest and more than held her own. But she'd been told Orion's speed was legendary. Poets sang of it.

Orion approached her and towered over her. "Do you still wish to go through with this?"

"Why? Do *you* want to back out?"

A few of the villagers chuckled, and Orion laughed as well. "I like your spirit, child."

Labrius cleared his throat, which effectively silenced everyone. Pointing to a rough, narrow road leading to the next village, he said, "The girl, Atalanta, and the hero, Orion, will race down that track." He cleared his throat again. "We'll place a marker two miles down, attended by a judge. Once they've reached the marker, they'll turn and run back. The first to reach the well will be the winner."

Looking down the long straight track, Atalanta again felt her heart sink. This was not how she raced Urso. They went through the forest—over trees and through rock clefts and wading across streams.

Suddenly that thought gave her an idea. Perhaps there was a way to even the odds just a little, to turn Orion's great size and strength against him.

"What sort of a race is that for a hunter?" she asked.

Orion raised an eyebrow.

"Does a hunter chase an animal along a straight flat track?" Atalanta continued. "Does a hunter run halfway then turn around and go back before catching the prey?"

Orion smiled. "What do you suggest then, little huntress?"

"Let's go through the woods," she said, gesturing toward the thick woodland to the north of the village.

"And what will be the object of the race?" he asked.

Squinting, Atalanta used the flat of her hand to shield her eyes from the sun. "What's that up there?" she asked, pointing. "Up on that hill beyond the trees."

Orion's sharp eyes followed her finger. "A statue."

"That's our shrine to Artemis," Labrius said.

"Make that our finishing post then," Atalanta suggested.

Orion smiled fully, showing his white, even teeth. "Agreed. The first one to touch the statue is the winner."

Atalanta nodded and held out her hand.

Orion took her hand in his but was careful not to squeeze her fingers too tightly. "It looks to be at least a mile and uphill the whole way," he observed. "Are you sure those spindly legs of yours will carry you?"

They must, Atalanta thought. *I have to be part of this hunt.* She swallowed hard.

The starter asked: "Are you both ready?"

Atalanta looked down at the ground. "Ready," she whispered.

"Let's get on with it," Orion said. "I'm growing hungry for breakfast."

They waited till the people of Mylonas had walked up along the trail and the finish line at the shrine was well watched over by Labrius and his council of elders.

When all was ready, the starter—who was Labrius' stoop-shouldered son—began his count. "One . . ."

Atalanta chewed her lip nervously. She needed to make a good beginning, for if she fell behind Orion at the onset of the race, she might never catch up.

"Two."

Orion did a deep knee bend.

I can do this, Atalanta tried to give herself courage. *He's too vain to believe it possible. He's never run with a bear.*

"Three . . ."

Atalanta felt as tight as a bowstring. *No,* she thought suddenly, *I am the arrow in the bowstring.*

"GO!" shouted Labrius' son.

Atalanta sprang forward at once, the arrow released from the bow.

Orion's start was slower as if he knew he didn't need to exert himself fully.

An enthusiastic yell went up from the crowd on the hill.

"Orion! Orion!" they cried. "Victory to the huntsman!"

Atalanta gritted her teeth, ignored their calls, and ran toward the trees, her legs pumping. She thought about keeping up with Urso, pictured him ahead of her, and raced to keep up.

"Run, Atalanta! Run!" It was Evenor. His voice floating down the hill was remarkably like her father's and his encouragement put an extra spring in her step. Surprisingly, she found herself in the lead. She didn't dare look around for fear of giving away as much as an inch.

Though he had started more slowly, the huntsman's muscular legs were now hurtling him forward in long, powerful strides that devoured the distance between them. Soon he was alongside Atalanta. "You're nimble, girl, I'll grant you that. But you've a long way to go. A start is not a finish."

Atalanta said nothing. She was saving her breath, straining every muscle to keep Orion from pulling away early in the race. But little by little he drew ahead.

Only a short way into the forest, Atalanta told herself. It was through the wild, forested country of the north that she'd raced Urso, and that experience was what she needed to give her a chance.

They ran under the canopy of the trees only a few feet from each other, passing from sunshine into leafy shadow. Ahead of her, Orion suddenly turned and plunged into a thicket of blackberry bushes, tearing a path through it like a bull trampling a hedge.

Atalanta rushed headlong through the gap he'd made, fighting desperately to catch up.

Now negotiating the forest's many obstacles became part of the race. Here alertness and agility counted as much as speed. Boulders blocked the way, trees tilted across their path, great holes in the ground yawned at their feet. All of these had to be swerved around, dodged, leaped.

They took separate tracks, Orion on the higher ground, Atalanta below him. He remained bull-strong, blasting through what couldn't be gone around. But Atalanta was deer to his bull.

It helped her to be the smaller now. She could duck

overhanging branches, slip through narrow slits in the rocks, and make sudden changes in direction more quickly than the big man.

She saw Orion as a flashing shadow moving through the trees, slightly up the hill and to her left. Gradually the gap between them narrowed and, as it did, they both came upon the same fallen tree trunk, lightning-struck and gaping. Leaping at exactly the same moment, they hit the ground on the far side together, matching step for step.

I've caught up! Atalanta thought. Thick sweat plastered her hair to her brow; her tunic clung clammily to her back. She was struggling hard to keep her breath steady and the blood was pounding in her temples. She could only hope that Orion was suffering as much.

Out of the corner of her eye, she saw him set his teeth in a grimace as he summoned another burst of speed.

Then his pace faltered.

A thick copse of trees was blocking their way. At the sight of it, Orion broke off and swept around to the left to try and bypass the obstacle.

Atalanta decided that this was her one chance to pull ahead. Running straight into the cluster of trees, she drove through the narrowest of gaps between them, tearing her tunic and skin alike as she scraped against the rough knobby trunks. A low branch raked across her head, another smacked her in the face, which brought tears to her eyes. But still she kept on, slim enough to slip through.

On she sped, her arms now thrust ahead to push other branches away from her face. Twigs and leaves snagged in her hair, but at last she broke free, bursting into a more open stretch of forest.

She could see no sign of Orion.

Where is he?

She didn't dare stop to look around in case he was already far ahead.

Then she heard him behind her, to her left, grunting like an angry boar. The sound drove her on as surely as a sharp spear in the back. Her legs were protesting now, telling her they had no speed left. She willed herself to ignore them.

She thought of Urso and how he ran so easily, eating up miles in a steady rolling gait. *Be a bear,* she told herself, and at that very moment she was a bear, her two legs feeling like four as she galloped along.

A wide stream suddenly stretched right across her path. She could hear Orion in close pursuit and knew that she couldn't afford to lose as much as a single pace.

Gathering her nerve, she jumped the stream.

Be a bird, she thought, willing her arms to be wings. But it was too far across. Her left foot came down in the water and slipped on a layer of smooth pebbles. She pitched forward, throwing her arms out to protect her face as she fell. She hit with a splash and her right knee scraped painfully over a jagged stone.

A huge shadow flew over her and Orion landed with

a thud on the far side. He swiveled around and looked down at her in triumph.

"You should go back to the village and have that tended to," he said, his words puffing out like strength ebbing. "Young pretty legs like yours shouldn't be scarred." *He was*, she thought, *older than he'd seemed in the village. Much older. Older than Evenor. Old as my father.*

He was bent over, breathing hard.

She thought, *Old man, this run has sorely taxed you.*

Gritting her teeth against the pain in her leg, she scrambled up onto the bank and darted into the forest.

Now the ground was rising toward the hill where the little shrine stood. Without warning, a high steep bank reared up in front of Atalanta, like a massive wave. She attacked it, grabbing onto handfuls of grass, roots, forcing herself upward. The grass on the northern slope was still slick with morning dew and the soles of her sandals kept slipping. She kicked them off and dug her toes into the ground, clawing up the rise like an animal.

Orion came charging after her and leaped, his hands catching hold of the top of the bank. But when he tried to pull himself up, his fingers slipped off the dewy grass and he slithered back down. Furiously cursing, he mounted a second attack, but he was too late.

Atalanta had already reached the top and clambered to her feet. From here the slope was less severe. She drove herself up, ignoring the spasms that shot like streaks of flame down her thighs and calves, the pebbles that dug into her bare feet.

Every breath she took was like a fire blazing through her lungs. A pain lanced through her left side as though someone were forcing a long sharp needle between her ribs. But worse than her own pain was the sound of Orion struggling behind her, his ragged breath like a roaring wind.

And then she was there—on the hilltop. At the shrine.

Ahead of her was the simple figure of Artemis set atop its crude pedestal of gray stone. The people crowding around it were shouting.

She couldn't distinguish the words they were saying, couldn't tell who they were calling for. She only had the wit to throw herself forward, flying vertically across the last few yards.

The crowd parted for her and her arm stretched out, fingertips brushing over the feet of the goddess. Then she hit the grass, bruising her cheek as she landed.

"You've won!" Evenor cried. Then to the suddenly silenced crowd, he called, "Atalanta won! The girl won!"

She turned over and saw his kind face looking down at her. He reached out with his hand and pulled her to her feet.

Orion erupted onto the scene, as furious as a storm ripping through a field of corn. He let out a wordless cry of anger that sounded like an animal's roar. Lashing out with one massive fist, he knocked the statue off its pedestal. The stone image of the goddess rolled across the ground several times before coming to rest face up in the grass, its stone eyes staring up at the blue sky.

Then Orion turned from the crowd, showing them his back, his shoulders heaving as he drew in a series of deep, calming breaths. When he turned around again, the smart of defeat was still smoldering in his eyes, but he had control of it.

"Game's over. Everyone back to the village," he said in a low rumble to the crowd. Then to Atalanta he added, "I guess, little girl, you'll be joining the hunt."

CHAPTER EIGHTEEN

THE ROAD
TO TEGEA

Orion seemed more than eager to set out for the palace of King Iasus at once. Atalanta was sure that part of his eagerness had to do with getting away from the scene of his embarrassing defeat, but she said nothing about it. In fact, she said nothing at all, eating the celebratory breakfast without speaking a word.

Orion took his meal standing, apart from the others. He even turned away several young men of the village who begged to join the hunt. He was so curt with them, they stalked away, cursing Orion angrily.

"Who does he think he is?" one of them said.

"Only an old man," said another.

"A slow old man," added a third.

Though she felt sorry for them, Atalanta kept her

silence. After all, those same young men had been Orion's greatest fans only hours before.

"You'll have a tale to tell, when you come back," Phreneus said to Evenor and Atalanta with an envious grin. Then he added, "Everybody in Eteos will give you all the wine you can handle just to *hear* the tale of Orion and the Arcadian Beast." His voice rose in its enthusiasm. "How he crept up on the mantiger and—"

"He hasn't killed it yet," Atalanta interrupted sharply, the first words she'd spoken since the race. "My father always warned me not to suck the marrow from the bones of a live beast."

"We're not doing this for wine," Evenor reminded him, "or for the tales we can tell. We're doing it for the good of our people."

"We're not doing it for Orion's glory either," Atalanta added.

As if called by his name, Orion suddenly appeared behind Evenor. "There's no glory for any of us till the beast is slain," he said. "Afterward, there'll be plenty to go around. Pick up your gear and let's be on our way."

Atalanta started to protest that he'd misunderstood what she meant, but he'd already gone back into Labrius' house. Shrugging, she picked up her gear and stood. Whatever appetite she'd had was gone, anyway.

Just then Orion came out of the house, fully armed. The two of them stared sullenly at each other across the courtyard. When Evenor joined them minutes later, they were still glaring like two boars getting set for battle.

"It's the mantiger we're after," he reminded them, "not each other."

Orion had the grace to look embarrassed, and Atalanta bit her lip before turning her head away. Hot tears stung her eyes and she blinked them away. The last thing she wanted was to be scolded by Evenor.

The entire village turned out to see them off. Orion's final wave of farewell was greeted with a cheer, except for the three young men who glowered in the back of the crowd.

"I don't mind telling you I'm glad to be away from here," Orion confided as they headed down the track. "There's nothing I find as wearisome as hordes of country folk demanding that I tell them stories of my adventures."

Atalanta covered her mouth with her hand to hide a smirk. Orion hadn't seemed to need much prompting to relate his stories.

Indeed, it wasn't long before he was telling Evenor and Atalanta all about a seven-headed sea monster he'd slain while on the island of Delos, about his faithful dogs who could put up ninety birds with one leap, about the Keshite lion he'd captured alive and given as a present to the king of that country, and so on and so on. If she hadn't seen him wrestle the raging bull to the ground, Atalanta would have thought he was making all of it up.

But maybe, she mused, *maybe most of it's true.*

When he was done storytelling, Orion spoke to them about the length of spears, the proper flight of arrows, and the best way to hold a lion's jaws apart. He pointed out tracks on the path, animal scratchings on the trees, and the difference between the scat of a stag and that of a doe.

The man simply couldn't stop talking.

Atalanta mentioned this to Evenor once, when Orion had gone on ahead to scout, and he replied quietly, "Perhaps he's lived too long alone in the woods and is used to the sound of his own voice."

She had no answer for that, nor did Evenor seem to expect one.

They walked farther, but now darkness was stitching up the garment of the day. Soon it would be time to make camp.

Spotting a rabbit lurking in the long grass, Atalanta took the bow off her shoulder and an arrow from the quiver, and in one swift movement bagged the creature.

Once they found a place to camp and had laid out the fire perimeter and the rabbit was cooking on a greenwood spit, Orion passed her his wineskin.

"Good shot," he conceded.

Atalanta's cheeks reddened, but she nodded her thanks. It was as if she and Orion had come to a kind of alliance. She smiled to herself. Rabbits were easy. Wait till he saw how she stood up to the mantiger's charge.

She went to sleep to the drone of Orion's voice, waking only when Evenor called her for her turn standing watch. Though with the din Orion made snoring, she doubted any animal—even the mantiger—would come near.

Over the next few days, Orion took it upon himself to instruct Atalanta in some of the finer points of hunting.

"A bow's fine for rabbits and squirrels," he told her, "but you need a proper hunting spear for bigger game."

"This has served me well enough," Atalanta said, patting her own light javelin.

"A weapon that does no more than wound can be the cause of your own death," Orion cautioned her. "Especially hunting boar."

She nodded. Her father had said the same.

"Boars die hard. Wounded, they're as vengeful as the Furies. Evenor can vouch for that," Orion added.

"I was young then," said Evenor, running a finger down the long white scar on his arm, "and too eager to claim a trophy."

"I *have* hunted boar," Atalanta started to say, but Orion continued as if she hadn't spoken.

"A wounded beast is more enemy than prey," he said. "If your shot doesn't bring it down, it's safer to miss altogether. If you're trying to stop a boar with that bow of yours, little huntress, don't aim for the heart. His hide is too thick and his breastbone will block the way. Aim for a vulnerable spot on the head: the eye or the ear. With a spot of luck you might pierce his brain. Otherwise that pretty skin of yours will get damaged."

Evenor moved between them and pointed at an old bite mark on Orion's left arm. "I see you've picked up your own share of wounds."

"As I said before, a man who flinches from danger is no hunter," said Orion. He pulled aside the lion skin and pointed. "See—there. And there. And there." Each place he touched was a fearsome scar, some puckered like little mouths, others long white slashes. "But there is enough danger in the wild without taking foolish risks, little huntress," he said, turning again to Atalanta. "No matter how helpless a beast may appear, don't hold back from a final spear thrust or you could pay with your life. And if you corner a beast in its lair, be prepared to strike without hesitation."

On the third night of their journey, during her turn at the night watch, a familiar scent caused Atalanta to stare nervously around before she realized it was the smell of bear.

Glancing over at Orion, she saw he was fast asleep and—for once—not snoring. Evenor also was deep in slumber.

Noiselessly, she slipped away from camp, gliding a short way through the shadows, before she found Urso crouched in the darkness. As soon as he saw her he let out a soft, welcoming growl.

"Hush, boy!" she whispered urgently, clamping a hand over his muzzle, "We can't let Orion know you're here. Who knows what he'd do."

Urso rubbed his shaggy neck against her.

"I've missed you, too," she said. "But we're going off to King Iasus' palace to round up enough men to hunt the mantiger."

At the beast's name, Urso snorted.

"No," she told him, "you can't come along. To Orion you're just a helping of meat and fine fur cloak."

Urso made a low, plaintive whine.

"Yes, it's dangerous," Atalanta confessed, "but if you want to help me, you have to keep out of sight. We'll be in Tegea, the king's city, soon. It won't be safe for you there, so you have to stay out here, in the forest."

Urso licked her hand.

"I can't go home until this is done. The mantiger killed my father and it's threatened my friends. We're connected somehow, that beast and me. I don't know why, but I know it's so."

She wrapped her arms around Urso's neck and hugged him hard before pushing him away. "Go now," she said. "I have to get back before somebody notices I'm gone. Besides"—she struck her fist to her chest—"I am standing guard."

The bear stood up till he towered over her. Then he

struck a paw to his own chest. Clearly he was saying that he, too, would stand guard. Then he bounded off into the trees, a great dark shape that was one minute there and the next gone.

Atalanta stood for a few moments, remembering the feel of the bear's head under her hand, the shaggy roughness of him. Then she turned to head back, and walked right into Orion, who was emerging from the bushes, his long spears in his right hand.

Atalanta leaped back in shock.

"I woke and you were gone," he said in explanation.

"I thought I heard something moving around. But I was wrong."

He narrowed his eyes at her. "None of us—myself included—is to leave guard station and go off alone." He paused and sniffed at the air. Then his eyes scrutinized the hard-packed ground carefully.

"Probably just a rabbit," said Atalanta, stepping into his way.

Orion lifted his head and raised an eyebrow. "A rabbit? With that musk?"

For a heart-stopping instant, Atalanta was afraid he'd insist on pushing past her, find Urso's tracks, and set off after him. But instead, Orion just turned around and headed back to camp. Letting out a sigh of relief, she followed.

CHAPTER NINETEEN

THE CITY

fter three days and nights, they passed beyond the trees and the green light of the forest, and came upon a long, parched road.

"A few miles up this road should be Tegea," Orion said.

"How do you know?" Atalanta asked.

"Look at the way the tracks of carts and horses go forward. The city calls them," he said.

Just then a cloud of dust came sweeping toward them out of the east. Atalanta could hear a great clattering of hooves.

"It sounds like a stampede of wild horses!" she cried.

Orion looked at her oddly. "Those are only chariots from the city."

"She has probably never seen a chariot," Evenor said. "I have only seen two in my life."

In fact Atalanta wasn't sure what a chariot was, but she'd never let Orion know that. Instead, she stepped to the side of the road and rested her hand lightly on her javelin.

As the dust settled, Atalanta could see that pairs of horses were pulling six small, open-sided, double-wheeled wagons, each carrying two riders made of bronze. The metal covered their chests and surrounded their heads, casting their faces into shadow.

Atalanta raised her javelin defensively. "What kind of monsters are these?" she whispered.

Orion laid a hand on her arm, forcing her spear tip down. "Not monsters. They're warriors. From Tegea. King's men."

The chariots pulled to a halt in front of them and one of the warriors climbed down. His bronze breastplate was inlaid with elaborate silver swirls, his helmet ornamented with a great crest. Removing the helmet, he walked over to Orion.

Why, Atalanta thought, *he looks quite normal.* The man seemed in his middle years, with curling black hair and a small dark beard. He gazed with steady gray eyes at Orion, at the double spears, at the lion skin draped over his shoulders.

"Stranger," he said, "who are you?"

"I am Orion, son of Hyrieus," Orion announced

grandly, striking himself on the chest.

"Orion!" exclaimed the man. "The gods be praised that our messengers found you. I am Ancaeus of Tegea, brother of King Iasus." He, too, struck his chest. "My men and I are patrolling the land to keep our people safe from the Beast of Arcadia. With you here, that will no longer be necessary."

Atalanta turned to Evenor and whispered, "What makes him think that patrolling the main road will keep the mantiger from their farmyards or fields?"

"Hush," Evenor replied.

"Take me to King Iasus," said Orion, "that I may offer my services."

"Gladly," Ancaeus replied. Then, as if only now noticing Atalanta and Evenor, he asked, "Who are these rustics?"

"My companions," Orion replied.

"What—even that savage-looking girl?"

Orion laughed. "Even her."

Ancaeus shrugged and waved them forward. "Climb aboard the chariots then."

Orion was to ride with Prince Ancaeus of course, while Atalanta and Evenor were to be with the soldiers in the following chariots. Atalanta didn't like the feel of the armor pressing against her or the men who looked at her as though she were some sort of rodent who had sneaked up between their feet.

The chariot started with a lurch, wheeling about so

sharply, she almost fell out. She had to cling to the light wicker frame as the leather straps that formed the floor swayed beneath her feet.

Down the wide road they sped, the horses kicking up dust. Atalanta bit her lip to keep from crying out. Her stomach felt as if it had fallen into her knees and was slowly trying to climb back to its proper place again. It was a long, uncomfortable ride, but the walk would have been longer. Atalanta wasn't sure which she preferred.

At last Tegea came into view.

Atalanta had never seen a city before. When she bothered to imagine one at all, she'd always assumed a city would look just like the villages she was familiar with, only with more cottages.

The reality was quite different.

A ten-foot-high wall surrounded a mass of brick buildings, many of them two and three stories tall. As the chariots passed through a gateway, armored guards atop the wall saluted.

"Hail, Ancaeus!" they cried.

In the streets people looked down at them from high windows and balconies. Some even walked on the rooftops as though they were walking on the clouds.

Surely this is what Olympus must look like, Atalanta thought, *the place where the gods live.*

They passed grain stores, smithies, bakeries, wine stores, stables, carpentries, and scores of other buildings she couldn't begin to identify. Wagons had to be wheeled out of the way as the chariots threaded through the crowded streets. Then the chariots turned onto an even wider street at the end of which rose an enormous building which had to be the royal palace.

Surely, she thought, *it's the biggest thing ever built by man.*

The palace was surrounded by a great wall. It had high towers and ramparts patrolled by stern-looking men in polished bronze armor with huge shields and long spears. The closer the chariots came to the palace, the more impregnable the place seemed.

At last, they pulled through the gates and into the palace courtyard. When she climbed down from the chariot, Atalanta felt her legs wobble unsteadily.

"Why have they put a wall around the city?" she asked Evenor once the queasiness in her stomach had passed. "Is it to keep the people from wandering away and getting lost?"

"Of course not," he answered with a laugh.

Atalanta was peeved at his response. "Well, that's why they pen in the sheep and goats back in Eteos."

"The wall isn't to keep people in," Evenor explained patiently. "It's to keep Tegea's enemies out."

"What sort of enemies?"

"Soldiers from another kingdom."

She gaped at him. "There are *other* kingdoms? Surely not as large as this."

"Larger," he assured her.

"Have you been there?"

He laughed. "I've never even been *here*."

She wondered that he was so calm about everything—the ride, the armored men, the high wall. Then another thought struck her. "Why would other kingdoms want to come here?"

He smiled at her and said softly, "Rival cities are like great bulls. Each one wants to control all the territory. So every so often they attack one another. That's why Tegea has walls."

She nodded thoughtfully, then said, "If the kingdoms could agree not to attack one another, they could save themselves a lot of bother."

Evenor put his head to one side, considering. "A queen couldn't have said better, child."

Just then Orion walked over, looking both proud and confident. "They're giving us quarters right in the palace where we can wash up before being presented to the king."

"Doesn't he know that you get dirty traveling in a chariot?" Atalanta asked.

"Hush," Evenor cautioned, but he was smiling.

Orion paid her no attention for he was already following Prince Ancaeus into the palace. Atalanta and Evenor had to move quickly so as not to be left behind.

The inside of the palace was even more astonishing than the outside. Atalanta found herself thinking how cold

and unforgiving the white marble floors were for someone used to the softness of grass or the straw-strewn
earth floor of a farmer's cottage. The walls of the palace
were also of smooth stone, but these were painted in
bright colors. Every few feet oil lanterns set in alcoves
gave out a weak, flickering light.

Suddenly the men were guided in one direction and
Atalanta was taken in hand by two women—servants by
the way they fluttered about—who insisted she go with
them.

"Or trouble be on our heads, mistress," confided the
younger.

They brought her up two flights of stairs to a small
chamber with a window that overlooked the courtyard,
then left. Atalanta ran over to the window, glad of the
open air. Glancing down, she saw the horses being led
off to the stables, the chariots rolled off into storage.
There was no way down from the window. It was too
high to jump.

I am here, then, so make the best of it, she told herself.
It was certainly better than being chained to a pillar in
the middle of a village. But somehow it felt even more
imprisoning.

She turned and went over to the bed, a high mound
of straw on a wooden platform. She set her weapons
down on the linen coverlet where they sank into the
thing as if into quicksand. She scowled. *Imagine sleeping
on that!*

Suddenly someone giggled behind her. She whirled around to see three new serving girls bustle into the room with bowls of water, towels, combs, and other implements she didn't recognize. The girls put these items down on the wooden table and surrounded Atalanta, clucking disapprovingly.

"We'd better get these dirty animal skins off," said one.

"And do something about this," trilled another, plucking at Atalanta's matted hair.

The third tutted. "It's going to take more than that to make this one presentable. Where *does* the king find them?"

Atalanta pushed them away.

"Keep your hands off me!" she roared, whipping out her hunting knife. "Get out! Now!" She slashed the air with her blade.

The servant girls ran screaming from the room, calling for the guards. Closing the door behind them, Atalanta went back to the window.

In a few minutes Evenor came rushing in and looked at the knife in her hand. "What's going on?" he asked. "I hear you tried to murder somebody."

"They attacked me," said Atalanta stubbornly. "They picked at my hair and poked me and . . ."

Evenor grinned. "I expect they were just trying to clean you up. Look, here's a bowl and cloth. Pretend you're by a stream and wash the dirt off your face and arms. Let the girls come back and help you get dressed."

"Why should I?" Atalanta demanded sullenly.

"Because you want to go on the hunt," Evenor answered.

"What does washing have to do with the hunt?" She felt hungry and angry and tired all in equal measure.

"It has to do with *royalty*, Atalanta," he answered with cold patience. "Kings appreciate washing and *this* king is putting together the hunt for the mantiger. Please him, and you can go as Orion's protégée. Fight him— and you're on your own."

She glared.

Evenor continued. "Look at me—I've already washed. Am I less a hunter? What's a little bit of water and a few fine clothes if it means we rid the world of that awful beast."

She ground her teeth in frustration, but she knew he was right.

An hour later they were walking to the throne room behind Orion. He was in a white chiton, cinched with a leather belt, the lion skin cape over his shoulder looking freshly brushed. His dark hair gleamed with oil and his sandals were oiled and polished.

Evenor was dressed in a simpler chiton, girdled at the waist with a woven belt.

At least they look comfortable, Atalanta thought. She'd been put into a short-sleeved gown that reached to her ankles. It kept catching between her legs, tripping her up. She could no longer stride as she was used to, but was forced to take shorter, mincing steps. She hated it. There were three gold pins in her hair.

As they walked down the hallway, flanked by a pair of richly-garbed courtiers, there were murmurs of admiration.

Gritting her teeth, Atalanta tried to keep up with the men and kept failing. A lock of her hair had come loose from one of the pins.

Evenor dropped back to walk with her.

"Remember, you have to bow before the king," he reminded her in a whisper.

She spit out a reply. "Why? Does he need to see the top of my head before he can talk to me?"

Evenor sighed. "Really, Atalanta, you're too stubborn for your own good. We have customs back in Eteos, too."

"Yes, I know, and they're just as stupid," she said. "Like making sacrifices to the gods when they don't really need anything we can give them."

Evenor groaned. "By Hermes, don't let the king hear you. They are big on sacrifices here."

"I don't much like gods or kings," said Atalanta, her voice tight. "And I don't mind if any of them know it." She remembered Pan laughing at her. "Not that they care."

A set of double doors opened before them, and they were ushered into the presence of King Iasus. Armored soldiers lined up along the walls, their spears held out at arm's length. A cluster of courtiers in colorful robes stood to one side of the king, whispering comments as the newcomers approached.

Orion fell to one knee in front of the throne where Iasus, his beard curled into tight dark rings, watched them.

"Welcome, Orion, son of Hyrieus," said the king, holding out his hand.

Atalanta felt a dig in her back from Evenor, but she couldn't move. Her eyes were fixed upon the great crimson banner hanging behind the throne. Emblazoned upon it in gold was the stylized image of a boar—exactly the same image as that on the ring that was hanging around her neck and hidden only by the flimsy bodice of her dress.

CHAPTER TWENTY

CHOSEN FEW

T he king clapped his hands, the sound echoing in the great hall. "A banquet for my guests," he called. "And send in the court poet."

Atalanta was relieved to hear there would be food, for they hadn't eaten a thing since arriving in Tegea. She sat where instructed, on a bench next to Evenor with a long table in front of them. To her right was a woman with a cascade of blond hair pinned up with a red flower who seemed to shrink away from her.

"I'm starving," Atalanta whispered to Evenor. She could hear her stomach growling. *Perhaps that was why the woman moved away.* It didn't matter. Once the food arrived, her belly would be quieted.

However, the court poet arrived first—a small

weasel-faced man, his skin as pitted as a stone wall. The food was delayed while he sang a poem in honor of Orion. His recitation went on and on, listing every beast Orion presumably had ever slain.

Even the king began to look bored. Or hungry. Or both.

When the song finally ended and the servants came in bearing great platters of food, the hall erupted into unrestrained cheers. *Less for the singer and more for the food,* Atalanta guessed, refusing to join in the applause.

Instead, she gazed up again at the royal banner above King Iasus. Fingering the ring under her gown, she hardly dared to imagine what connection there was between herself and the royal house of Arcadia. *Would the king know?*

Iasus suddenly laughed uproariously over some joke of Orion's. The king's laugh was loud and grating.

Atalanta's hand fell to her lap. Surely there was *no* connection at all. If she showed the ring, they'd all laugh as loudly as the king. Or arrest her for theft.

Putting all thought of the ring aside, she turned to Evenor. "You'd think Orion would get tired of the fuss they make over him."

Evenor shrugged. "What else is there for him? He has no home, no family."

For a moment she stared at Orion across the table. *No home and no family,* she thought. *How much we have in common.* She hadn't considered that before.

Helping herself to a handful of olives from a wide platter, she washed them down with a sip of wine from a long-stemmed cup. She was just reaching for some bread when a young man two or three years older than she leaned over her shoulder. Pulling away from him, she scowled, but he just smiled in return.

"You're the wild girl, aren't you?" he asked. "I've heard them talking about you."

"They should find something else to talk about," said Atalanta. "Or you should find something else to listen to."

He laughed. "They've plenty of other things to talk about," he said. "And most of it not worth repeating."

She must have looked surprised, for he smiled again. "I see you agree with me."

"I think I'd better keep my mouth shut. Except for eating," she answered, ostentatiously popping another olive between her lips.

"Good advice, I'd say, though others at court won't." He smiled. "I hear that you attacked the servants with a knife when they tried to wash you."

"I would have—but they ran away."

He laughed again. "I think I would have, too!" His eyes were merry and the color of olives. "My name's Melanion, son of Amphidamas. I'm one of the royal cousins." He swept back a shock of black curls that had fallen across his brow.

Atalanta reached out for another olive. "That must

be nice for you," she murmured. Then it occurred to her that this might be her one chance to find out some more about the royal house, so she softened her voice. "If you're one of them, then tell me who they are."

"I suppose living in the woods, you wouldn't have much chance to know who's who." He smiled again. He seemed a young man of many smiles. He pointed to the king. "That's Iasus, of course. To his right, beside Orion, is the king's brother, Prince Ancaeus."

"I've met him," said Atalanta impatiently.

"Not long out of the woods and already an expert!" Melanion sounded as if nothing she said could insult him. "The woman on the king's left is Queen Clymene and as you can see, soon to have a child."

Atalanta stared intently at the royal group, and as she did so she felt again the cold metal of the ring against her skin. Dared she suppose she might be one of them? Would she even *want* to be?

"Do they have any other children?" Atalanta inquired lightly, trying her best not to sound too interested.

"No," Melanion replied, helping himself to one of the dates from her dish. "Though there was a rumor that . . ." For a moment he paused, than smiled again. "Everyone thought she was barren. So many years and no child. They wondered if the king would put her aside. But instead he called in a mage from the East, a Phoenician priest of the goddess Astarte. Within months, the queen was blooming. And the priest, for all his help, was sent home, his pockets—they say—bulging with gold from the royal coffers."

"How do you know all this?" Atalanta asked.

He shrugged. "I'm a royal cousin. We hear all the best gossip."

She made a face at him. "If you're a cousin of the royal house, shouldn't you be sitting up there with the rest of them?"

Melanion shook his head. "They don't actually care much for me," he said, sweeping his unruly curls back. "They consider me a troublemaker."

"Then go and trouble someone else," said Atalanta, chewing on her bread. She doubted he had anything else of interest to tell.

Ignoring her, Melanion squeezed onto the bench beside her. "They say you were raised by wolves," he said amiably.

Atalanta gazed studiously in the other direction. "Bear."

"They say you live out in the wild and eat nothing but snakes and honey."

This time she didn't answer.

"They say . . ."

She turned on him. "*They* say an awful lot, don't they."

"I like traveling about in the wild, too," Melanion went on. "I don't like being cooped up in the palace. I like to get out in the mountains and the forests."

"I don't do it because I like it," said Atalanta. "I do it because . . ." She found herself stuck for a reason he could understand, adding lamely, ". . . because it's the only way I know how to live."

Melanion's face became serious. "It must be nice, though, not to have your father forcing you to come home, making you live up to your responsibilities."

Atalanta felt a sudden pang of loss. "I don't have a father. He was killed by the Arcadian Beast. And since you like traveling so much, why don't you go!" She gave him a shove with both hands and sent him sprawling.

Undaunted, he got up and knelt beside her, suddenly serious. "I'm sorry about your father. I didn't know. And as for going—well, that's the very point I was getting to." He took a deep breath and said in a rush, "I thought you might put in a good word for me with Orion. You know, get him to take me on the hunt."

"I don't have any good words for you," she said, and deliberately turned her back on him. "Go and talk to him yourself." This last she said over her shoulder.

At that moment King Iasus stood up. "A toast," he declared, raising his cup, and all eyes turned to him. Even Atalanta's. "To Orion, the greatest of all hunters, the savior of Arcadia."

"Orion! Orion! Orion!" It was a tide of voices as Orion's name passed from mouth to mouth across the hall. Cups were raised in his honor.

After swallowing a draught of the wine, King Iasus looked around at his people, a long, lingering gray-eyed gaze. "And now, brave hunters of Arcadia, which of you will accompany the great Orion on this quest?"

For a moment there was silence. Then every man in the room leaped up, yelling out his name, calling to Orion. The women applauded and threw flowers at Orion's feet.

Orion waited, hands across his chest, till the tumult ended. Then he said, "Noble king, this beast has proved as elusive as it is deadly. If we send an army against it, it will simply run off to terrorize a different part of the kingdom. And our great force will be too encumbered to catch up."

The king had his hand on his cheek and looked deep in thought. He nodded at Orion's words.

"A hunt," Orion continued, "is best carried out by a small party, a half dozen at most. They must be woods-wary and smart. They need courage, caution, and a good nose for game."

"Then take Nicon!" someone cried. "He's got the biggest nose."

A laugh ran around the room and the man named Nicon made a rude gesture at his tormentor. It drew another laugh.

Atalanta ignored the others, thinking: *Orion is right.*

At once the Tegeans started calling out again.

"Me! Take me!" cried one man, his right arm in the air.

"I'll go with you, Orion!" cried another, standing.

Others leaped up, too, including the large-nosed Nicon.

Orion raised both hands in the air to silence them.

"I have already chosen my hunting party," he said. "Firstly my companions, Evenor and Atalanta."

"A girl!" Prince Ancaeus erupted indignantly. "You refuse the army of Tegea and take a half-wild girl in its place?"

"That's *my* choice," said Orion, staring the prince down. "I judge her worthy of a place in the hunt for my own reasons. You, of course, may come also, Ancaeus, to represent the royal house of Tegea. The king has told me of your eagerness."

This appeared to mollify the prince, who fell silent and returned to his wine.

"To complete our company we'll be joined by Hierax, the royal huntsman," Orion announced. He gestured toward a hawk-faced man with a gray beard who was seated a few places to his left. There was a muted cheer from around the hall, but it did nothing to disturb the grim set of Hierax's features.

Melanion was on his feet like the rest of the Tegean men. Suddenly he vaulted onto the table in front of Atalanta, knocking her dish of fruit to the floor. "And me!" he cried.

"Get down!" Atalanta yelled at him. "You look like a fool."

He whispered to her, "You said to talk to him myself."

Orion looked vaguely amused. "And who might you be?"

Melanion pushed back his unruly hair once more. "Melanion, son of Amphidamas, your honor, kinsman to the king."

"The king might as well be kinsman to a donkey!" Ancaeus bellowed disdainfully. "You empty-headed vagabond, what use are you?"

"No one knows the lay of the land like I do," Melanion asserted confidently. "I know every rock and tree of Arcadia as well as you know the inside of a wine cup, Uncle."

"Why you arrogant stripling!" Ancaeus roared, leaping to his feet and drawing a knife.

In one swift motion, almost too fast to see, Orion had whipped the knife out of the prince's hand and tossed it onto the floor. "Be seated, my lord," he said. "Remember your royal dignity."

Ancaeus bit back his anger. Slowly he sat down again.

"I've been seeking out birds' eggs and following deer trails since I was an infant," said Melanion. "I've traveled from one end of Arcadia to the other and never taken the same route twice."

"Yes, to the despair of your father," said the king, drawing a round of good-natured laughter from his subjects.

"This land is unfamiliar to me," Orion mused, rubbing his chin, "and a good hunter relies on good information." He turned to Hierax. "What do you say, royal huntsman? Can the boy be of use to us?"

"It's true he's traveled far and wide. Poked his nose where even shrews and weasels don't go," Hierax answered slowly. "Blindfold him, stop up his nose and ears, he could still find his way by the feel of the ground beneath his feet."

"Better than you, Hierax?" Orion asked.

The old huntsman took a moment to answer, glancing grimly at the king first. "I know the royal hunting grounds better than any man alive," he said. "But outside of that, the boy knows best."

Atalanta looked at Melanion with different eyes now. She jumped to her feet. "This mantiger is no respecter of property," she said. "King's land or farmer's land is all the same to him. I say we take Melanion, too." Then her cheeks reddened and she felt a sudden fever rushing to her brow, so she sat.

Orion laughed. "Well said, my little huntress. I was thinking the same." He turned to Melanion. "You can come, too, boy. But understand this: You obey my commands and go nowhere unless I tell you to."

"I shall be as obedient as a hound," said Melanion with a bow.

"And I hope as much use," Atalanta muttered behind his back. And when he turned and winked at her, the

flush—which had only been on her cheeks and brow—
spread throughout her body and she feared she might be
sick on the spot. So she left the room without so much
as nodding at the king.

CHAPTER TWENTY-ONE

SECRET TEMPLE

T hat night, asleep in a soft royal bed, Atalanta was visited by a dream. Like a voice in the wind, it called her from her room, beckoned her through the door and out into the hall. Strangely, there were no guards or servants to be seen, as if everyone in the palace had suddenly disappeared.

Atalanta felt herself being drawn mysteriously to a dark staircase that went down and down to another passage. This in turn brought her to a spiral stair that descended into a damp and gloomy underground chamber that was lit only by a few oil lamps set in alcoves in the walls.

Silently, she followed the lamps to a door that was standing ajar. She could hear voices on the far side of the door but couldn't tell who they were.

Slipping through the doorway, she found herself in an enormous domed room, the ceiling rising high overhead, with huge supporting pillars of stone.

From the safety of one of the pillars, she peeked out and saw King Iasus pacing. His face was flushed and sweating, and he clenched and unclenched his fists with great agitation.

Looming over him in the center of the room was a statue of a woman at least fifteen feet high. Her eyes and mouth were brightly painted and cow horns stuck out from the golden ringlets of her hair. Her belly was hugely swollen, and below it her stone skirts stretched to the floor in folds of purple and crimson. It was the goddess Astarte.

"What else was I to do?" he protested. "I prayed to you and to Demeter and even to Hera, queen of the gods. But you gave me no help!" He seemed to be talking to the empty air, not to the statue in front of him.

And the empty air answered him.

"You were a fool." A woman's voice filled the chamber like the soughing of the wind. "By your own choice you dishonored the gods of Arcadia, making sacrifices to this painted statue of a foreign deity."

"All I wanted was a son," Iasus insisted, raising his arms above his head as if entreating the air. "To carry on my name and my line."

"Did you really think you could call on barbarian

gods and not pay a price?" the voice demanded, rising like a winter gale. "It is you, Iasus, who called down this curse upon your kingdom."

"I sent the Phoenician priest back to his own land," Iasus pleaded. "Can't you, in turn, Great Artemis, send the beast back from whence it came?"

There was a silence as deep as doom and then a sigh. Atalanta leaned forward to hear.

"But you kept the statue. The beast," Artemis informed the king, "comes from the same desert lands as does this barbarian goddess. A fitting punishment for your sins, Iasus, and your pride."

"Can't you stop it, O Artemis?"

The air seemed to draw itself up. "Stop it? Why should I?" The voice laughed cruelly. "No man is ever cursed unless he brings it down upon his own head. This is the price you pay for invoking foreign gods and practicing their vile rituals, Iasus. This beast will destroy you and yours, and your kingdom will be brought to ruin."

Iasus shook his fist at the air. "Never. The great Orion is here now. He'll kill the beast."

"Only your own blood can save the kingdom now," the voice said coldly. "Orion has his own sins to pay for. He, too, has dishonored me."

Atalanta thought suddenly of Orion pushing the statue of the goddess to the ground in his fury at being beaten in the race. *Oh no,* she thought, *he was sorry right after. Don't punish him, Great Artemis, for that. But she didn't dare say it aloud.*

All at once the statue of Astarte began to sway, leaning from one side to another, almost drunken in its movements.

"Let this be the last time Astarte shows her painted face in Arcadia," proclaimed the voice.

The statue began to fall forward and Iasus leaped aside, then ran for shelter behind a pillar.

When stone hit stone, the statue broke into hundreds of pieces that rolled across the floor. The noise of the impact echoed over and over in the great chamber.

Atalanta sat upright in bed, the echoes still crashing in her ears. Her heart was pounding. The dream had been so real, yet here she was safe in the silence of her own bedchamber.

Was it the rich food that had caused her night visions? Or the suggestion of the rumor that Melanion had told her?

Or was it something else?

She slid out of bed and put on her hunting clothes. Grabbing up her bow and quiver of arrows, she padded out of the room. She followed the corridor as she'd done in her dream. Sure enough, it brought her to a stairway. And the stairway to the passage and the spiral stair.

She knew then that below would be the lamp-lit tunnel and the great domed room. *How could I have dreamed all this?* she wondered.

Facing a wounded boar was nothing compared to the fear she felt now. She took a deep breath, brushed aside an impulse to turn and run, and started down the spiral steps.

Just as in the dream, the door to the domed room was ajar. She stepped inside without making a sound. The sight that greeted her made her catch her breath. There was a man crouching among the shattered fragments of a statue, examining the pieces.

But it wasn't King Iasus.

It was Orion.

She thought she'd been silent, but he suddenly said without looking up, "Little huntress, what brings you here?"

She opened her mouth, closed it, opened it again. "A dream," she said at last, painfully aware of how foolish she sounded. "I saw the king here and the statue fall." She said nothing of the goddess. Nothing of Orion's fate. It had been a dream after all, and she knew she was no oracle.

Orion stood and looked strangely at her. "I came because my instincts told me the king was hiding something. Something important. One should never go on a hunt unprepared." He stopped as if expecting some response from her.

She nodded.

"I couldn't sleep," he continued, "thinking about what it might be. I walked the corridors and heard the sound of breaking stone, which led me to this place." He picked up a painted fragment from the floor. It was an eye, heavily outlined in black, the eyelid painted green. "I've seen such images before, in the temples of the distant East."

"Is it . . . is it a goddess?" Atalanta asked, already knowing the answer.

He nodded. "Astarte at a guess. The goddess of childbirth."

"And the beast is terrorizing Arcadia because of her?" Atalanta asked.

Orion tossed the stone aside. "Whoever or whatever brought the mantiger here, it's still only an animal. And I have never met an animal I couldn't kill." He smiled grimly at Atalanta and walked out of the room.

Remembering the cold voice of the goddess in her dream, Atalanta shuddered. She was amazed that she found herself afraid for Orion.

And for herself.

CHAPTER TWENTY-TWO

THE GREAT HUNT BEGINS

Orion insisted on leaving at dawn. Only a few servants were bustling about at that time, more interested in their work than the hunting party gathered in the courtyard. The majority of the Tegeans were still sleeping off the banquet.

Prince Ancaeus looked as if he wished he were still abed. He wore a rough tunic, dyed green, like his nephew and Hierax. But while they were both clear-eyed, his eyes were rimmed with red and his face pale. Atalanta worried about him. A hunt was no place for a sick man.

"Perhaps we should carry you in a litter, Uncle," Melanion suggested with a smile.

Ancaeus merely glowered. "Where are the chariots?" he complained. "Why aren't they ready yet?"

Leaning patiently on his spears, Orion cast a disapproving eye over the battle-ax Ancaeus carried. It had a broad, curved blade and a three-foot-long wooden handle. "You'd be better served by a hunting spear, my lord," he said. "You can't keep an animal at bay with that. It'll have your arm."

"Keeping it at bay isn't the point, is it?" Ancaeus retorted. "And a spear point can be deflected too easily." He ran a finger down the edge of the axe. "This will shear through flesh and bone like a scythe cutting corn at harvesttime."

"The prince likes to deliver the killing blow," Hierax explained, his voice carefully neutral.

Suddenly Atalanta understood and felt sick with the knowledge. Ancaeus wanted to wait until his huntsmen had the mantiger helpless before he went anywhere near it. But as the ranking noble, he would insist on the honor of killing the beast for himself. She wondered briefly what Orion thought of such a plan. She thought she could guess.

There was a brief flurry at the entrance to the palace, and King Iasus appeared with his queen.

In the weak morning light, she realized that there was something familiar about the queen, something about the eyes and nose that she hadn't noticed in the firelight.

But I never met her before yesterday, Atalanta told herself. *What is it that's so familiar?* Then she realized that she'd seen that same coloration, those same olive-shaped eyes, the same tilt of nose whenever she bent over a pool of water and beheld her own reflection.

Atalanta turned away from the royal family and shook her head. *No,* she scolded herself. *This is only imagination, Atalanta. The royal couple had no children. Melanion said so and surely he would know.*

"You have decided where to begin the hunt then?" King Iasus asked Orion.

"Yes, Hierax and I have been going over the various sites of the attacks," Orion replied. "Here, sire, is a rough map of what we know." He drew on the loose ground with his sandal. Atalanta had never seen any such thing before, and it looked like nothing more than a squiggle of lines.

"See, Your Majesty, there is a pattern to the way the beast kills," Orion said. "There. There. There. There. There." His sandal pointed out places on the rough map. "It moves out of the southwestern mountains, north-ward around the kingdom, then back again to the south. After that there is always a lull. The beast's last kill was here." He jammed the butt end of one of his spears at a point about a hand's span from Eteos. "Knowing the pattern will let us find him."

Squinting her eyes, Atalanta tried to understand what the men seemed to know. The pointed shapes Orion called mountains, the circles for Tegea and Eteos, the snaking lines of road and river, and the northern movement of the beast. *I must learn more about maps,* she told herself. *I'll make Orion teach me.*

Orion continued, "The mantiger and creatures like it always have a lair, and in this case I am guessing it's in the mountains of the southwest. Melanion tells me that there are many caves there." His sandal touched the leftmost area of the squiggles.

Suddenly the whole thing made sense to Atalanta.

"That's where we'll have our best chance of catching up with the mantiger," Orion said.

"While it's denned," Atalanta whispered to herself.

"Succeed in this and any reward you care to name will be yours," said the king, leaning in close to Orion and speaking in a low voice. "Just remove this curse from my kingdom."

Queen Clymene left her husband's side and walked toward Atalanta with an expression of grave concern on her face.

Does she recognize her face in mine? Atalanta wondered. The thought actually alarmed her. How could she like this queen, if it turned out she was the one who'd left Atalanta on the hillside?

"I am unhappy that this girl should be going on such a hazardous expedition," said the queen to Orion. "She's far too young."

"It was her own choice," Orion said, "and I can't deny her a place in the hunt. It's a point of honor."

The queen reached out a tentative hand to touch Atalanta's hair. "Men and their honor." The queen sniffed. "As if being a hero was all there is to life." She turned to Atalanta again. "Then, child, you must make the decision for him. The slaying of the mantiger is best left to these hunters. There is no need for you to go. You're no Artemis. We have quarters here in the palace where you can stay until your friends return."

Atalanta recoiled from the queen's touch, her heart hammering in alarm. All at once the palace seemed like a trap to her, one that would spring shut and keep her forever from the woods she loved.

"No, I'm going with Evenor and Orion," she said abruptly. "I belong with them. I don't belong here."

The queen looked by turns angry, puzzled, and hurt by the hostile reaction. She turned to her husband. "Iasus, can't you . . . ?"

The king waved her aside with a movement of his hand. "This girl's fate is no concern of ours," he said as the chariots arrived.

"Here are our rides," said Evenor.

"Good," Atalanta said. "Now the hunt can begin." *Even riding in a chariot is better,* she thought, *than facing the mystery that lies here in Tegea.*

Orion turned to the king and queen. Striking himself on the chest with his fist, he proclaimed, "I, Orion, son of Hyrieus, dedicate this hunt to you, King Iasus, and all your kingdom."

Everyone cheered.

The journey to the southwest lasted two bone-wrenching days that took them through fertile valleys where fields of corn danced in the breeze. They drove past wandering herds of cattle and flocks of sheep and groups of scampering goats. They wound through stands of oak, fir, and cypress, and had to ford two small rivers. It was Melanion who knew the way.

When they finally reached the foothills of the southwestern mountains, the hunting party dismounted, leaving the charioteers to return to Tegea.

Atalanta wasn't sorry to see them go.

Each member of the hunting party was to carry packs of food and lengths of rope and cord to fashion into snares. Prince Ancaeus was none too happy about this, even though Hierax had volunteered to carry much of his equipment and Melanion took over the care of his uncle's food.

"Ah, Uncle, as the poet sings—I'll be ant to your grasshopper," Melanion said, laughing.

"We could have brought servants to carry all of this for us," Prince Ancaeus pointed out.

"More mouths to feed," said Orion. "More feet to give us away with a careless step." He turned and added under his breath so that only Atalanta, who was standing by his side, heard, "More idiots to protect."

She was shocked at what he said, more shocked because she agreed with him.

"So what do we do now?" Evenor asked, coming over

to Orion. The others joined him.

"Spread out into a line, twenty yards between each hunter," said Orion. "We'll move up into the hills looking carefully for any sign of our quarry. Watch out especially for tracks, spoor, a feather from one of its wings. Look out for any animals that have been savagely butchered, their hair and teeth, and bones."

"What if we spot the mantiger itself?" asked Melanion, who was chewing on a stalk of grass.

"If that happens, then scream for me," Orion ordered emphatically. "And quickly!"

"I shall be quickness entire," Melanion responded. "Shall I take the right flank?"

Orion shot him a hard look. "Now, keep in contact with those to either side of you by calling out at regular intervals. At noon, when the sun is high in the sky, we'll gather together to make reports and eat. Then we'll resume the search."

By afternoon Atalanta was beginning to wonder if Orion had made a mistake. For all the tales that were told about him, he was still just a man and as likely to be wrong as any other. Certainly she'd found nothing to indicate they were on the mantiger's track. No prints, no feathers, no spoor. And more importantly—no butchered animals. At noon the others had reported the same lack of success.

She could only hope that some other member of the party would pick up a trail by nightfall.

All at once she heard a movement behind her. She waited, pretending to be unaware of its approach, then spun around in an instant, spear poised to throw.

"Melanion!" She lowered the spear but kept the spearhead pointed at his middle. "Of all the muddleheaded . . . Why are you sneaking up on me?" she demanded. "You should be checking your patch of forest."

Melanion shrugged. "All I've come across out here are some bees and a few mice. Have you found anything?"

"Only an idiot who should be tethered up for his own safety." She walked briskly on, eyes scouring the ground on either side. Melanion jogged after her.

"You know, there's something familiar about you," he said, popping a fresh stalk of grass into his mouth and chewing on it thoughtfully. "When I first saw you at the banquet, and then again the morning we left, when you were talking to the queen, and now looking at you in this light, I have a strange tickle at the back of my mind. Something I see but yet don't see."

Atalanta could feel her face flush. Unaccountably her hand was clenched tightly around her spear. Too tightly. Carefully she loosened her grip. Lightly, she said, "Did you come to chase the beast or to hound me?"

"Madam, I am wounded by you," Melanion answered. "As the poet says, a man wounded by a rabid dog sees the beast's image in all waters."

"I don't know your poet, but I'm no mad dog," she

answered. "Except that I'm mad at you for interrupting me. Now will you go back to your line?" She strode quickly away to resume her part of the search.

As evening fell, the hunting party gathered to discuss their progress. No one had come across any sign of the mantiger.

Ancaeus looked around at the tree-covered slopes, the forbidding crags, the sun setting behind the looming western peaks. "We should have brought more men," he complained. "We are too few to cover all this ground. Isn't that right, Hierax?"

The royal huntsman nodded reluctantly, bound by duty to agree with his prince, but he said nothing. Atalanta doubted he'd spoken more than a few dozen words since they'd left Tegea, but he'd never strayed far from Ancaeus' side, as though he were intent on guarding the prince, either from the dangers of the wild or from his own folly.

"The mantiger can only be in one place at a time," said Orion, "so we only need to cover one place."

"We've hardly seen any kind of animal at all, let alone the one we're looking for," said Ancaeus. "Perhaps this is the wrong place."

"That's the whole point," said Orion. "Sometimes you find tracks or spoor, other times it's what you *don't* find that leads you to your prey."

Ancaeus looked baffled. "What's he talking about?"

Evenor answered, "This place should be rich with animals—deer and boar and rabbits and birds. Yet there are none. What Orion means is that the mantiger's scared them off."

Orion turned to Melanion. "You said there are caves up here."

"Yes, lots of them," said Melanion, pointing toward the mountains. "I've found mountain cats and bear and—"

Prince Ancaeus interrupted. "You're no hunter, boy. A sluggard, yes. A parasite . . ."

"I'm not a hunter, Uncle, but I *am* a finder," Melanion said.

"Yes, you find, then you run away."

Orion raised his hand, which effectively stopped their quarreling. "Let's make camp," he said. "Any family feuds should be settled at home, not here."

They set down their equipment in the shelter of some poplar trees, and Orion gave Melanion the job of gathering firewood with Hierax to guard him.

Atalanta was glad to see him sent off on an errand for she was afraid he might start questioning her again. Sitting down on a stone, she set her quiver and bow aside. Then she began rubbing her temples for she'd developed an ache that seemed to invade both sides of her head.

"Something's troubling you," Evenor said. "Is it Melanion?"

"He keeps following me around."

Evenor chuckled. "You'll soon have lots of young men following you around."

"They won't if they know what's good for them," Atalanta said. "But that's not what's bothering me. This is something about King Iasus and his brother."

"What do you mean?" Evenor squatted next to her so that they were face-to-face.

"Well, you've heard Ancaeus complaining, haven't you. He sounds like he doesn't want to be here at all. So why did he come?"

Evenor ran his fingers through his hair. "I think he wants the glory of the hunt but none of the hard work or discomfort."

"Maybe," Atalanta said. "But I can't help feeling that the king *made* him come." She remembered Artemis' voice in her dream saying, "Only your own blood can save you now."

"Why should you think that?" Evenor asked.

Not wanting to tell him about her dream or the rumor or the statue or the image on the ring, she stood up. Head aching, she picked up her bow and started toward the trees. "I think I'll make some use of the last of the light."

She didn't expect to find anything—and she was right.

CHAPTER TWENTY-THREE

ATTACK

The morning dawned drearily with gray clouds rolling in from the west. By the time they had eaten the food they'd brought with them, a light drizzle was pattering on the leaves.

Rain didn't disturb Atalanta. Living in the wild she'd hunted in worse conditions than these. She supposed, however, that Prince Ancaeus, used as he was to the comforts of the palace, would be complaining bitterly to anyone who would listen. She just made sure she wasn't near enough to hear.

As the day wore on, the rain grew heavier, until by afternoon they were surrounded by a cold, dank haze. Atalanta realized that it would be hard enough to find one another in this weather, let alone an elusive and deadly animal.

Orion's voice sounded through the trees, calling the hunting party together, and slowly they gathered in a small clearing, damp and disheartened.

A flash of lightning ripped across the sky, followed by a long, slow rumble of thunder.

"This is getting us nowhere," said Orion. "We'd best find shelter and resume when the rain eases off."

"The wet earth will at least show up any fresh tracks after the rain stops," said Evenor with what sounded like faint hope in his voice.

"Like these you mean?" Melanion was crouched at the edge of the clearing, poking in the sodden grass with his finger. Orion reached him in two strides and squatted beside him.

"Some sort of large animal has been here all right," Orion said. "Though it's hard to say what."

Hierax knelt down and ran his fingers over the grass but offered no guesses.

Atalanta didn't look at the tracks. Instead she'd been examining a nearby tree. "Look at these grooves in the bark here," she called.

Evenor joined her. "Claw marks."

Orion got up and went over to examine the marks through narrowed eyes. "Bear?"

"Look how big they are, and how high," Atalanta pointed out.

Some of the scratches were higher than the top of Orion's head.

"An animal's been sharpening its claws here, a big one," said Orion. "Could be bear."

Hierax and Ancaeus, too, examined the marks. The hunter smiled. "There's fresh mud smeared on the bark from the pads of its paws."

"That means it was just here a short time ago," said Evenor.

A sense of imminent danger sent a prickling sensation down the back of Atalanta's neck. She turned in a slow circle, her spear clenched tight, her ears alert for any sound of movement in the gloom. All she could hear was the rain beating on the foliage and the tense breathing of her companions. All thought of shelter was forgotten now. Each of the hunters held their weapons ready.

"Do you think it knows we're here?" Ancaeus asked anxiously, shifting his axe nervously from hand to hand.

Orion shook his head. "This is an animal, not a fiend. Let's see if these tracks lead anywhere. And friends, let's be silent about it." He held up his hand and motioned them behind him while he scrutinized the ground.

Step by careful step, he followed the wet tracks, bent over in concentration.

All of a sudden he stood up and spat to one side. "Pah! The tracks give out after only a short way. All of you, make a tight circle around these tracks and then slowly spread out to check the rest of the clearing."

As they began to move into the circle, Orion added, "Stay alert."

Atalanta wiped a wet strand of hair from her face and cried out a single word, "Wings!"

Everyone stopped, turned, looked at her.

Orion smacked a hand to his head. "Of course! I'm so used to tracking large animals on the ground, I'd forgotten . . ."

At that very moment there was a blast of lightning. It lit the clearing and silhouetted a huge winged shape that swooped down out of the storm-torn sky. A hideous roar shook the air as the mantiger crashed into the middle of the hunters, its wings and paws and snaky tail striking out in every direction.

Caught unawares by the suddenness of the attack, the hunters were sent flying like dice tossed from a cup.

Atalanta was struck across the face by a slash from the snake tail and went sprawling onto her back. She was saved from further injury by her pack. Even dazed, she had the presence of mind to roll away, out of reach of the beast's claws. Over and over she rolled until she bumped painfully into a tree, bruising her ribs.

Another roar rang in her ears, drowning out the cries of her companions. Groggily she forced herself to her feet and looked around for her spear.

Melanion staggered toward her, a wide gash in his head. Atalanta grabbed him to keep him from falling over.

"Where's your spear?" she asked urgently.

"Lost it," he croaked, face screwing up in pain.

"Banged my head on a rock."

Atalanta wiped the raindrops from her eyes as another lightning flash illuminated the scene. She saw the monstrous shape of the mantiger crouching over Ancaeus who was sprawled on his back in the grass, eyes wide with panic. He had his axe in his right hand.

Atalanta tried to move toward the fallen prince, but Melanion was still leaning on her and the added weight made her slip on the wet earth and collapse to her knees.

By now Ancaeus had pushed himself up on his left elbow and lashed out with his weapon. The blade whooshed through empty air, missing the mantiger completely. Before he could attempt another blow, a massive paw slammed his arm to the ground and pinned it there, the claws going right through the muscle.

He screamed.

Hierax rushed out of the gloom, limping, and drove his spear at the creature's flank, but a wing swept up and batted the weapon out of his hands.

"Don't fear, my prince!" Hierax shouted, drawing his knife. Before he could strike, the monster rounded on him, seizing him in its yawning mouth. Still pinning Ancaeus under its paws, the mantiger shook Hierax like a cat with a rat, till his neck cracked. Then the beast flung the lifeless body to the ground.

It was then that Orion charged, yelling a war cry as he came at the beast with his first spear.

The mantiger twisted with astonishing speed. Pulling its claws out of Ancaeus' arm, it grabbed the shaft of Orion's spear between its teeth. With a jerk of its huge maned head, it tried to rip the weapon out of Orion's grasp, but the huntsman held on fast. He planted his feet firmly on the ground, his muscles swelling as he tried to lever the spear away. He swatted at the beast with the second spear, for he hadn't the distance to throw it.

Scrambling about on her hands and knees, Atalanta groped for her own spear, wondering all the while where Evenor had gone to. Beside her, Melanion was crawling, trying to shake the pain from his injured head.

The mantiger pushed toward Orion, lashing out at him with its claws, and Orion managed to dodge the blow by less than an inch, losing the second spear in consequence. Then the beast flung back its head and the spear was wrenched from Orion's hand. He was thrown back, colliding with a boulder.

The mantiger spat out the spear as though it were a piece of straw and let out an awful roar. Step-by-step it began to advance on Orion, snarling its victory.

At last Atalanta's fingers closed around a shaft of a spear, one of Orion's. She jumped to her feet and threw it. But she wasn't used to its length or heft, and it struck the beast on the shoulder and glanced off harmlessly.

Still, for a split second, the mantiger was distracted and that was all the time Orion needed to yank out his long hunting knife. He struck out at the beast with a wide swing of his arm. The blade only cut through its heavy mane as it drew back with a growl.

Evenor suddenly appeared from behind a bush where he'd been hurled in the initial attack. Blood gushed from a wound in his arm, but he rushed to Orion's side and for a moment held the mantiger at bay with his spear.

"Get the prince away!" Orion ordered the others as he scrambled up. Then he and Evenor slashed and jabbed desperately to hold off the ferocious creature that was slowly forcing them back.

Now Melanion was on his feet and, together with Atalanta, he hurried to his uncle and grabbed him under his arms. Heaving Ancaeus to his feet, they dragged him into the trees. As soon as they did so, the mantiger whirled about, left its pursuit of Evenor and Orion, and bounded after them.

Atalanta looked back over her shoulder and saw the mantiger getting ready to leap.

Suddenly from out of the darkness, a wild, shaggy shape threw itself at the mantiger.

"Urso!" Atalanta cried. "Don't! Stop!"

But he wasn't hers to command. Bear and mantiger were of a size and they fought viciously, rolling over and over in the wet grass.

"Go!" Orion shouted at Atalanta and Melanion. "Get

the prince away from here."

Atalanta hesitated a moment. How could she leave her bear? She felt for her bow and arrows. Miraculously they were not damaged. But in this light, the chances of hitting the bear rather than the mantiger were great. She didn't know what to do.

Melanion was dragging his uncle by himself now, and they were nearly into the trees.

Think, Atalanta, think, she told herself. There was nothing she could do for Urso at the moment. She *had* to help with Ancaeus. She ran over and grabbed his other arm.

"More men," the prince was mumbling to himself as his feet trailed across the ground. "Should have brought more men."

"Over that way," said Melanion. "There are some rocks there. We can barricade ourselves in if necessary."

In a few minutes they'd reached a cleft in the rocks with a broad stony overhang extending above. This formed a small shelter at the foot of a crag that soared above them as a sheer wall. They stepped over an enormous fallen tree to get into the cleft.

Then they laid the prince on the ground and looked out through the gap in the rocks.

"Listen!" said Melanion. "I think I hear something coming!"

Atalanta listened. She heard deep breathing and the

sound of little rocks scattering away from heavy feet. Setting an arrow to her bow, she crept out till she could see over the tree but not be seen and watched the wet foliage shaking violently. Whatever was coming up those rocks, she was ready to shoot.

CHAPTER TWENTY-FOUR

NIGHT

Lowering her bow, Atalanta gave a sigh of relief. The noisemaker was Orion, with Evenor close on his heels. Both men had grazes and cuts all over their arms and legs. Evenor's tunic was torn almost in two and blood was trickling down his leg as well as his arm. But somehow both men still had their packs and their weapons.

"Thank the gods you found us!" Melanion exclaimed.

"Two of you dragging a wounded, bleeding man," said Orion as the hunters squeezed through the cleft. "You weren't difficult to track. Even at dusk and in the rain." He glanced around. "You did well to find a defensible position."

"It was Melanion who found it," said Atalanta.

Orion grunted approval. "That overhang will not only shelter us from the rain, but will also keep the mantiger from attacking from above."

"And the gap can be easily defended," Evenor added.

"What about Urso?" Atalanta asked anxiously. "What happened to him?"

Orion looked puzzled.

"The bear," Evenor explained to Orion, then turned to answer Atalanta. "He was badly scratched and bitten, but when I glanced back, he was running off into the trees and the mantiger didn't seem to be going after him."

"You *know* this bear?" Orion asked, his eyebrows making mountains of surprise.

She nodded. "Of course he ran off. He only came to protect me."

"And a good thing, too," said Evenor. "Without his help, I doubt any of us would have escaped."

"We need no help from an animal," said Orion with a scowl as he gathered what little dry tinder was about. He added some larger branches from the fallen tree. Then he made a quick fire, sparking it with an extra spear point against his whetstone.

When the fire was going, he knelt over Ancaeus, who was curled up into a ball and moaning. Roughly pulling the man's arms away, he examined the prince's injuries.

"You'll live," Orion said, "but you'll be no more use to us on this hunt."

He took out his sleeping roll and cut it into strips with his knife. Then he used the strips of cloth to bind up the prince's more serious wounds and, with what was left, he bandaged Melanion's head.

"Perhaps my uncle was right," said Melanion gloomily. "Maybe we should have brought more men along."

"More men, more dead," Atalanta said.

Orion stood up and stretched his great muscles. "The girl is right. We would have fallen all over one another in that small space." He was silent for a moment, then said with brooding determination, "The beast took us by surprise. Tomorrow we'll surprise it. First thing in the morning we'll dig a pit, set snares, lay out bait. It won't find us napping this time."

"A pit?" Atalanta couldn't believe it and shook her head. "A pit won't be any use against a flying creature."

"That thing may have wings," Orion explained slowly, "but it's still big and heavy. It takes time and effort to get aloft at that size. You've seen its tracks. It walks more than it flies."

"But Atalanta has the right of it," Melanion said, glancing her way. "Even if it falls into the pit, it will fly right out."

Evenor understood first. "It won't have room to stretch its wings."

Nodding, Orion added, "And we must make sure it doesn't live long enough to try."

Ancaeus groaned. "Waste of time. That thing can't be

killed by normal means."

Atalanta was inclined to agree with him. The one thing that kept bothering her, though, was why the beast had attacked them at all. That hadn't been its way before. It had killed her father when he threw a spear at it, and maimed Goryx when he'd bumbled into it. But now it had changed its hunting pattern, which was strange indeed. And if it had attacked once, it would do it again. She couldn't see it waiting for them to dig a pit. The question was—who was it after? And why?

Ancaeus groaned again. "We're all dead, I tell you."

But Orion had had enough of Ancaeus. "Has the last of your feeble courage ebbed away, Prince?"

"Courage has nothing to do with it," Ancaeus said, trying to sit up and failing. "Don't you understand? This is the will of the gods."

There was a long silence in the cave until Atalanta stood and went over to stand next to the fallen prince. "You know why the beast is here, don't you?"

Already pale from loss of blood, Ancaeus turned pure white and averted his face from the others. He groaned as if in great pain. "My brother angered the gods. He told me that the beast won't disappear until it has been bought off with our family's blood."

Only your own blood can save the kingdom now, the words of her dream.

"I thought the beast seemed to be going for you," said Evenor.

"That's why Hierax was watching over me," Ancaeus said. "Iasus ordered him to."

Orion reached over and pulled the wounded prince to his knees. "It's time for the whole story, Ancaeus. We've been battling half blind. Tell us everything you know."

Ancaeus groaned again and closed his eyes. "More than a dozen years ago," he began, "Queen Clymene fell pregnant. Iasus was overjoyed and awaited the birth of the son who would inherit the kingdom. When instead the child was a girl, he raged against the gods and sent Hierax to put the child out on the mountain, saying, 'Let the gods save her or let her die. Her fate isn't in my hands but theirs.' He told the queen the child had been stillborn and, indeed, that was the story everyone heard, but the gods knew the truth."

Hierax! Atalanta thought, her whole body cold. *Had he hung the ring around her neck so that if she survived she might one day reclaim what was hers?*

Melanion had been keeping a watch out the front of the cave, but now crept closer. "This isn't a story I know, Uncle."

"It was hardly a tale the king wanted told," the prince said. "But Clymene wept for so many days, that Iasus' heart was softened and he sent me along with Hierax to retrieve the child. When we got there, no trace remained of the infant, but there were bear tracks all around the spot. Obviously she'd been killed and dragged off."

Now Atalanta felt hot and then cold and then hot again.

"Uncle, that's an awful story," said Melanion. "A girl child abandoned by a distraught father. But—it all happened years ago. What has this to do with what's going on *now*?"

Orion had taken to pacing in the small space. "Yes," he growled, "what has it to do with the mantiger?"

Ancaeus sank back against the wall. "What is time to the gods? They laugh at our calculations."

"Go on, go on," Orion said, losing patience with the prince.

Ancaeus wiped a hand across his mouth before continuing. Then, clearing his throat, he said, "For the next thirteen years, Iasus' efforts to produce a son came to nothing."

"The beast," Orion snarled. "Tell us of the beast."

Ancaeus nodded. "I am getting there. The story is unfolding. Iasus prayed to all the gods, but still Clymene remained barren. Then one day a stranger arrived at the palace, a traveler from Phoenicia in the East, an oily and disreputable creature I thought, but Iasus was taken by him. The man said he was a priest of the dread Astarte, a goddess of fertility and childbirth. He told Iasus that if he built a shrine . . ."

"Arrrrrr!" Orion bent, picked up a small rock, and hurled it angrily at the wall. "I have seen this shrine. And the ruined statue of Astarte."

"It was Artemis who smashed it," Atalanta said, the words seeming to come out of her mouth on their own.

They all turned to her, staring.

"How do you know that?" Melanion asked.

"I . . . I dreamed it," she said.

"Dreams—pah!" Orion spit to one side.

"But my brother had a dream, too," Ancaeus said. "Artemis came to him and told him that because he had worshiped a foreign god, the whole kingdom would be punished. She said only his blood . . ."

". . . could save the kingdom," Atalanta finished for him. She leaned toward him. "That was in my dream, too."

"But what does it mean?" Melanion asked.

"Iasus thought the dream was quite clear," Ancaeus told them. He was sweating now, for the fire had quite warmed up the cave. "He said it meant that only one of his kin can kill the beast. So he sent me to do it, having no closer blood relative. But I have feared all along that Artemis really meant that the beast can only be destroyed once Iasus and all his blood are slain."

"The gods always speak in riddles," Evenor said. "It pleases them to puzzle us."

"You all put too much credence in the gods," Orion said. "There is nothing they can send against us that can't be stopped by one good spear thrust." He stared at each of them in turn, as if daring them to argue with him. When no one did, he slowly nodded, satisfied that he'd established his authority.

"Now eat," he said, "and get some sleep. I'll take the first watch and the last. Atalanta will take the second watch, Evenor the third."

"I can take a turn," Melanion said.

"We need strength at the door and a huntsman's eye," Orion said, his voice coldly distant. "I judge that you have neither."

"But . . ."

"And you are also one of Iasus' blood," Atalanta said.

"Oh!" Melanion suddenly looked shaken.

"I am the leader," Orion added. "And therefore I make the rules. And no one—" he glared at Melanion— "*no* one has the right to question me."

No one did.

"In the morning," Orion finished, "I'll give each of you your tasks and we shall finish this business at last. This I promise."

CHAPTER TWENTY-FIVE

ONE SMALL
DEATH

T he thunderstorm was passing now, but even as the clouds cleared, night rolled in across the wine-dark sky. Atalanta found a spot in the cave across from Melanion and next to Evenor, and circled it like a dog getting ready for sleep. Ancaeus was stretched out at her feet, dozing fitfully, exhausted by his wounds.

Lying down across the entrance to their little den, his spears on his lap, Orion was clearly ready to defend the gap should the mantiger try to take the cave.

Atalanta's mind was reeling, her thoughts flying about like leaves in a gale. She'd suspected the truth of her parentage the moment she'd seen the royal banner. The queen's face in the morning light had confirmed those suspicions. Still Atalanta had refused to really credit such a possibility until now.

Now she could look away from the truth no longer. Iasus was her father, Queen Clymene her mother, and the child in Clymene's womb was her brother.

But how could she love them when they had given her away with such ease? Her real mother and father were the ones she'd buried by the little house in the woods.

She thought about all this muzzily, fighting sleep; but eventually sleep won the battle, though it was a sleep haunted by dreams. In her dreams Atalanta saw Queen Clymene lying prostrate on her bed, hands across her milky breasts, weeping for the loss of her child. She heard the baby on the hillside crying out in hunger and in fear, its wails growing louder and louder until she was startled from her dream by the noise.

Only then did she realize that what she was hearing was no dream-child at all. It was the sobbing of a grown man.

She sat up quickly in the half dark, wondering who among them could be weeping so. Prince Ancaeus in pain? Melanion in fear? Evenor missing his family?

"What's wrong?" she called out.

"Are we being attacked?" That was Evenor, his voice fuzzed by sleep.

"Atalanta, is that you?" Melanion called.

Prince Ancaeus struggled up, leaning heavily on one arm. "What? What? What?"

The awful cries went on and on.

There was only one of them left who hadn't responded.

"Orion!" they all said together.

The great hunter, clutching his head and screaming in pain, was suddenly outlined against the lightening sky.

"Aieeeee! Aieeeee!"

It was an awful cry that echoed inside the little cave until it sounded as if his voice were coming from everywhere. He stood shakily, lurching from side to side, slapping at his right ear, shaking his head till his hair stood up like flames.

"Aieeeee! Aieeeee!"

He bounced against the stone walls, staggering as if drunk, his limbs trembling.

"Aieeeee! Aieeeee!"

Then all at once he fell to the ground and lay still.

"Orion—what is it?" Melanion scrambled toward him.

But Atalanta was already there at the body, cradling Orion's head in her lap. She watched as a small shape dropped past her arm and scuttled away across the ground. Holding out her hand, she stopped Melanion from coming any closer.

"Scorpion!" she cautioned, setting Orion back down on the stone floor and standing up carefully.

It was the most dangerous kind of scorpion, its back marked with a pattern of green and red, and its tail the length of her hand. The deadly stinger was curved forward over its body, twitching, as if looking for another victim.

"Keep still!" she hissed at the others.

Pulling out her knife, she waited for a second, then leaned over and drove the blade right through the scorpion's jointed body, impaling it. Its pincers and eight legs wriggled helplessly until Melanion picked up a rock and crushed its head with a single blow.

Evenor hurried over and put his ear to Orion's mouth, listening for a breath that didn't come. Atalanta laid a hand over his heart. She couldn't find any beat.

They sat in that attitude for almost an hour, silent, not knowing what else to do. Then dawn broke across the valley and by its light they could all see that Orion's ear was red and swollen and his face discolored with the scorpion's deadly poison.

"It must have stung him in the ear while he slept," Atalanta said.

Evenor spoke in a harsh whisper, "We came to kill a mighty monster, but the mightiest hunter has been killed by one of the smallest creatures on the earth."

"One great man, one small death," Melanion said.

"But why . . . ?" asked Evenor.

Indeed, why? Atalanta thought. *Why should he have been the one punished? He* didn't have any of Iasus' blood.

Suddenly she remembered her dream in the palace, how Artemis had said that Orion had his own sins to pay for. Was this what she meant?

"Orion was our hope," groaned Ancaeus getting to his knees. "Our *only* hope. What are we to do now?"

"The first thing we must do," said Atalanta, "is to give him the proper honor." She struck her breast with her fist. "I, Atalanta, daughter of the forest, sister to the bear Urso, will avenge your death, Orion. I dedicate this hunt to you and to my father, who also died because of the king's sins."

The others struck their own chests and said similar words. It was little enough that they could do. Then, when the sun had risen fully, they buried Orion under a cairn of rocks within the cave, to keep off the wild beasts.

Evenor spoke a brief prayer before they left. "May this hunter's brave soul pass peacefully from the world."

Atalanta noticed that he'd said nothing about the gods. *Just as well,* she thought bitterly. *For this is their fault, and none of ours.*

CHAPTER TWENTY-SIX

ALLIES FROM THE WILD

"The hunt isn't over yet," Atalanta said, looking out across the valley. She was thinking about the goddess's words to Iasus. Perhaps if only royal blood could slay the beast, and she was a true daughter of the king, she could kill the thing. Hadn't she wounded it once already? Hadn't it flown off when her knife had cut it?

"There are only four of us now," said Melanion. "And Uncle is in no shape to fight. Think, Atalanta—what chance do we have?"

She turned around and glared at him. "As much chance as any hunter with courage and wits at her command. We can't quit. We owe it to Orion to go on."

"Besides," Evenor said sensibly, "what other choice

do we have? With Ancaeus injured, we can't move fast enough to escape."

Ancaeus winced as he tried to move. "Leave me," he said hoarsely, "for what good it may do."

Atalanta shook her head. "Orion never would have abandoned a helpless man. Neither shall we."

"You're right," Melanion agreed. Glancing quickly around the little den, he added, "I suppose we could hole up here and defend ourselves till Uncle Iasus sends men to find us."

"Not soon enough to do any good," said Evenor.

"Or I could go back to Tegea for help," Melanion added. "I'm a strong runner."

"That beast has taken deer and boar who run faster than you, my young friend," Evenor told him.

The air in the little den suddenly seemed hot and thick. Tempers were on the edge of flaring, dry kindling ready to ignite at the least spark.

"We came here to kill the mantiger," Atalanta reminded them, "and that's what we're going to do."

"With *what?*" Melanion asked. "We lost half our weapons running away from it. We've only three spears between us."

"We still have our knives," said Evenor, "and Atalanta's bow."

Atalanta looked at Orion's cairn. An idea had occurred to her, a foolish one perhaps, but one that might give them a chance.

"We won't just use weapons," she said. "We'll use the wild itself to help us. But first I have to find Urso."

"Your pet bear?" Melanion asked doubtfully. "How do we know where he is?"

"He was badly scratched and bitten when he ran off," said Evenor. "We don't even know if he's alive."

"He's alive," Atalanta insisted. "I'd know here if he were dead." She put a hand to her breast. "And he *will* help us." She paused and turned to Melanion. "Didn't you say you came across some bees back there?"

He shrugged. "Yes. There are plenty of them in this part of Arcadia. The gods alone know why. The land is poor enough."

"Good," Atalanta said. "Now—both of you—empty out the packs," she said. "I'm going to need them all."

"To do what?" Evenor said.

"You'll see." She grinned at him.

Exchanging puzzled glances, Evenor and Melanion began turning the packs upside down and dropping empty wineskins, ropes, knives, dried olives onto the floor.

"Are you all mad to obey her?" Ancaeus croaked. "She'll be a single bite for that beast."

"I've been a hunter all my life," said Evenor, "and Atalanta still knows more about the woods than I ever will. If there's a way to survive this and kill the mantiger, she's the one to do it."

He handed his empty pack to Atalanta.

"Thank you, Evenor," she said quietly. Then, taking all the packs and her bow and knife, and without further farewells, she slipped through the gap in the rocks.

The sky above was a pale blue without a single cloud. Sun-cast shadows made creatures where there were none. Crouching low, Atalanta ran swiftly down the rocky scree and into the forest, alert for any smell or sound or sight of Urso. She knew he would be close by.

She found Urso only an arrow shot away, curled up inside a thick clump of bushes, licking his many wounds. She was distressed to see the tears the mantiger had made in his flesh. There were bare patches of red, raw skin where whole clumps of his fur had been ripped out. Deep scores were gouged into his back.

"Oh, Urso!" she gasped, throwing her arms around his neck.

The bear licked her face in return and the two of them nuzzled and patted each other, growling softly.

"You trailed me all across Arcadia, you foolish, foolish bear," Atalanta said. "You saved us all."

Urso's growl turned to a plaintive whine.

"I know you're hurt," she said, tears running down her cheeks. "But I need your help. Remember how we used to go hunting for honey? How I had to run from the bees?" She made a buzzing noise and formed her fingers into flying insects, nipping at her own skin.

Urso gave a snort of recognition.

"We have to hunt for honey again, Urso. We need to find some beehives."

The bear shook himself all over, as if just rising out of a river, and padded out of his hiding place. He bent his head into the crook of her arm and she gave his ears an affectionate scratch, carefully avoiding a deep wound near the right ear. She hoped Urso and she could accomplish their task before the mantiger found them again.

The search for bees took the rest of the morning. With Urso's sensitive nose sniffing out the sweet scent of honey, Atalanta was able to fill the three packs with full hives, using a long forked stick to lift each hive out of the bole of a tree.

There was no sign of the mantiger, but neither she nor Urso relaxed. Even when they were concentrating on the bees, they kept alert to both sky and ground.

But both of them were breathing hard now, the bear because of his wounds and Atalanta because she'd been stung several times on her arms. They were tired, hungry— and hurting. Atalanta knew there was little point in pushing further. They needed to head back to the den where the others waited.

As they turned to go, Atalanta spotted a gleam of silver through the trees. "Look!" she said.

Urso's head jerked up and saw where she was pointing.

It turned out to be a small pool. Urso plunged in as

if he knew that his wounds needed to be clean, especially the ones he couldn't reach with his tongue.

Atalanta was more cautious, unwilling to put herself at a disadvantage in the water, but she bent down for several long draughts. Afterward, she made compresses from the muddy banks of the pool and covered her stings with them. The mud was cool and eased the pain. Then she filled her wineskin with fresh water and picked up the packs once more.

Suddenly a savage roar reverberated over the woody slopes.

"Come, Urso," Atalanta called, "we've got to get back to safety."

The bear needed no urging. Lunging out of the pool, he clambered up the banks at a run. Then, side by side, they raced through the woods till they got to the bottom of the scree beneath the cliff shelter. There they stood, catching their breath, the bear's sides heaving with the effort.

Realizing how exhausted Urso was, Atalanta stopped him there.

"Wait here. Stand guard," she said. "Growl if you smell anything coming. No need to make the climb unless you have to."

She left him and went quickly up the scree, darting into the cover of the rocks and calling out as she went, so they'd know she wasn't the monster.

When she reached the entrance to the little cave, with

the three packs over her shoulder, Evenor and Melanion recoiled from the angry buzzing.

"Are those bees?" Melanion asked.

She nodded.

"You *are* mad."

"We're hunting something that can fly," Atalanta replied matter-of-factly, "and as we can't fly ourselves, we need some help."

She raised the bags up, and the men flinched as the buzzing grew more furious.

"Just don't let them loose in here," she warned, "or we'll be stung to death before the mantiger can find us."

"We heard it roaring," said Evenor. "It's out there looking."

"We're not going to wait for it to come to us," said Atalanta. "Here, drink this and listen to my plan." She gave them sips from the wineskin and outlined what she had in mind.

"It gives us a chance," Evenor commented when she'd finished, "and we can't ask for more than that."

"We still need something to use as bait," said Atalanta. "Something to lure it out."

"A goat? Or a deer? Some game it can try to take from us," asked Melanion.

Evenor shook his head. "The mantiger's scared off any animals in this part of the forest."

"You can use me," said Ancaeus in a pained, hoarse

voice. As he spoke, he pushed himself to his feet, his back pressed against the rocky wall.

"Are you sure?" Atalanta asked.

Ancaeus' lip twisted in a sneer. "Do you think you've more courage than I, little girl? Do you think I want to lie here, cringing in fear, until I die of my wounds?"

"Uncle . . ." Melanion began, reaching out a hand.

Ancaeus slapped his arm aside. "Let the beast come for me. Better to die a man than live a coward. Just remember to have the poet sing about my bravery."

"You understand the plan?" Atalanta asked.

"A fool's plan," he replied scornfully. "But the only plan we have."

"I intend to kill the mantiger," Atalanta told him firmly, "and *not* at the cost of your life."

"Then make sure your aim is true," Ancaeus said.

CHAPTER TWENTY-SEVEN

THE TRAP

A talanta already had a spot in mind. It was on an animal trail leading to the pool that she and Urso had just left. There was enough dense greenery for the hunters to hide in and enough open ground for them to set their trap.

"Can you walk, Uncle?" Melanion asked.

"With your help," Ancaeus replied.

They all left the shelter of the little den, going carefully down the scree and then quickly along the path. Atalanta took the lead with an arrow in her bow. By her side ambled the bear. Next came Melanion, holding up his uncle with one hand, a spear in the other. Evenor was in the rear, and he had both spear and knife at the ready.

When they got to the track, Atalanta signaled them to stop.

"First we need to dig a trap," she said.

She and Evenor and Melanion took turns breaking up the ground with their spears, one always on guard.

As soon as he understood what they were doing, Urso pushed into their midst and began ripping up clods of earth with his long, sharp claws. He worked with furious determination, flinging piles of earth in all directions. The others helped to widen the hole until it was just large enough to hold their prey—but just.

Then Evenor and Melanion set about plaiting together branches and leaves to make a covering for the pit.

Meanwhile Atalanta took Urso with her and walked up the trail to where she planned to set her snares.

Urso was limping badly now. She ran a hand over his torn and matted fur, careful not to touch any of the wounds directly.

"I don't know what we would have done without you," she said.

He turned and gave her face a long, lingering wet lick, almost blinding her.

Suddenly a wild figure leaped out in front of them and Atalanta reeled back, stifling a scream.

"Pan!" Atalanta said. "You . . . startled me."

Stamping his goat feet, the figure grinned. "That's why they call it *panic*," he chortled. "I do so love to see mortals jumping out of their skins."

"Every time I see you, I think it's a dream. But I am wide awake this time."

He laughed. "Do I look like a dream?"

"Actually more like a nightmare."

He laughed again.

"Are you here to help us kill the mantiger?"

Pan stopped dancing and put on an exaggeratedly sad face. "Oh no, little huntress, I can't take a direct hand in any killing. Not I."

"Well, look what the mantiger did to my Urso."

"That's the point," said Pan, spinning about and then leaping to where Atalanta was and pushing his face right into hers. His musky smell at such close quarters was overwhelming. "Urso is the very reason why I've come."

Suddenly terrified, Atalanta moved away from Pan and threw an arm around Urso's neck. "*Now?*" she asked weakly.

"I told you before, the time would come for him to follow his own path," said Pan. "He's followed yours long enough, denying the impulses of his own nature to do so. But this is no longer his fight. It shames you to make him part of it."

Atalanta looked at the open wounds and listened to Urso's weary panting. Truly, she feared for his life.

She nodded reluctantly at Pan and turned to the bear. "You've done enough, dear friend," she whispered into his ear. "You've done a dozen times more than enough."

Urso nuzzled her and growled.

"No, I mean it. Truly I do." She pushed him away. "You have to go now. It's my destiny to be here, not yours."

He growled again.

She pulled him back and kissed him on the brow.

He whuffled.

Turning away so the bear couldn't see her tears, she told Pan sternly, "You take good care of him and guide him safely home."

Pan gave her a mock bow. "My word is my bond," he said, "which is more than *some* gods can say." He stretched out a hand toward Urso, and the bear padded slowly to his side. Then he touched Urso on the head and a great glowing, buzzing mist seemed to reach out and surround them.

As Atalanta watched, they turned and walked off through an arch of birches and out of sight.

Atalanta choked back the tears that were threatening to overwhelm her.

"Why now?" she cried, but could think of no answer.

When she returned to the others, the cover of intertwined branches had been finished and laid over the pit. Melanion and Evenor were even now spreading loose earth over it to further disguise the trap.

Ancaeus was sitting on the ground, holding one of

the spears as if guarding the other men. "Where's the bear?" he asked.

"He's done his part," Atalanta answered. "He's on his way home."

"So it's just us now." Melanion squared his shoulders, but his voice was unsteady. "Funny, I was counting on that bear!" He smiled, a shadow of his usual broad grin.

She nodded. "Have you heard anything?" She looked at Evenor carefully.

"Not a sound," he said. "You?"

"Nothing." She turned to Ancaeus. "Are you ready, my prince?" She held her fist to her breast to show him honor.

If he noticed, he didn't say, but he struggled to his feet, tottering a few steps toward her. He handed her the spear.

They took him by the arms then, helping him around to the far side of the pit. Here the trees grew too close and thick for the mantiger to attack from any direction other than directly across the trap.

As he settled his back against a tree trunk Ancaeus drew his long hunting knife. "I wish I had my axe," he said. "Then I might yet strike a blow that would do for that monster."

"No single blow will stop him," Atalanta told him. "It will take all of us working together." She didn't say that she doubted the prince had the strength to wield his axe, even if he'd had it. *How hard it must be for him to have to rely on us to keep him from harm,* she thought, adding aloud, "Though I, too, wish you had your axe. It had a fine sharp edge."

They walked away from Ancaeus carefully, skirting around the very edge of the pit.

"What do we do now?" Melanion asked, pushing his hair back from his sweaty brow.

"Conceal ourselves as best we can," Atalanta replied. "And wait."

She found a large acacia bush and hunched down behind it with a bag in front of her containing one of the beehives. The buzzing was more subdued now, as if the bees had resigned themselves to their prison.

Off to her left was Melanion with another of the bags, hunkered down behind some berry bushes. To her right, barely visible among the foliage, Evenor knelt and waited.

Only Ancaeus was in plain view, their human bait.

Atalanta checked her bowstring to make sure it was taut, then slid her knife out of its sheath and into her waistband. As she was without the spear she'd lost in the mantiger's first attack, these weapons would have to serve. She was too small to handle Orion's spears. It was best the men have them.

Time dragged on, limping toward sunset. The blue of the sky began to redden, like the skin of a ripening fruit.

Atalanta took a small drink of water from her wineskin and chewed on some berries she'd picked up along the way. They were early berries, tart and tasty, and seemed to explode in her mouth. All the while she never took her eyes off of the prince.

Ancaeus' chin was resting on his chest and his eyelids had begun to droop. *It might go easier for him if he falls asleep,* Atalanta thought. The waiting was bad enough for all of them, but it must be even worse for him, in the open, exposed on purpose to danger.

She heard a rustling to her left and immediately set an arrow to the bowstring.

It was only Melanion crawling toward her, looking as if he wanted to talk. She hissed angrily at him and waved him away.

Reluctantly he crawled back.

Atalanta shook her head. Melanion seemed to be finding it harder to sit still than any of them. *He'll never make a hunter,* she thought, then laughed at herself. *As if that were his one desire!*

Just then she heard another sound, a slight crackling, like a paw on leaf mold. She stared around but could see nothing. Yet somewhere in the forest—she was sure—a large animal was stalking them, waiting for dark. She knew it by the way everything went suddenly quiet—insects, small birds, even the trees seemed to be holding their collective green breaths.

Head snapping up, Ancaeus, too, was suddenly alert. He reached for the knife in his lap and the blade glinted dully in the last bits of sunlight slanting through the trees.

Suddenly, the greenery between Atalanta and Evenor burst apart. The mantiger—its wings tucked close to its body—was racing straight at Ancaeus.

The prince tried to brace himself, but the beast was almost on him. All he managed was a weak cry. "For Arcadia!" And raised his knife.

The mantiger snarled and leaped, landing at the far edge of the lattice of branches. For a moment nothing happened. The mantiger prepared to leap again, but—with a sharp snapping sound—the latticework gave way beneath its paws and it tumbled backward into the pit with a roar of outrage.

Atalanta, Evenor, and Melanion jumped out of hiding and ran over to the pit. Down below, the mantiger had righted itself, but as Orion had known all along, it couldn't unfurl its wings in the small space. Frustrated, furious, the beast was roaring and trying to leap up, but its great wings kept catching on the sides of the pit and knocking it down again.

Holding the bags by the bottoms, Atalanta, Evenor, and Melanion shook out the hives into the pit. The hives struck the beast's back and broke apart like ripe fruit, releasing the buzzing swarms.

Like a miniature army, the bees struck at the first enemy they could find. Pouring angrily over the mantiger, filling the air with a deafening hum as they attacked, they stung it again and again. The mantiger clawed futilely at them, tossed its massive orange head to get them out of its ears, its mouth, its eyes, the soft, vulnerable spots, which they seemed to find with unerring accuracy.

Maddened beyond endurance, the mantiger roared in pain and frustration, but the more it roared, the more the bees found their way into its open mouth. Clawing its way up the side of the pit through the cloud of insects, the mantiger finally got to the top. Its wings opened with a loud snapping sound and it tried to take to the air, still screaming its fury. The bees followed it out of the pit and continued their assault with renewed frenzy.

Atalanta fitted an arrow to her bow and fired. It struck the beast in the haunch but didn't penetrate far. The mantiger's skin was thick, but still she could see a bit of blood seeping from the wound. The scent of it made the bees even more frantic.

Ancaeus was on his feet now, eyes blazing feverishly. Fear and anger drove him, lending him strength. His right arm went back and he threw his knife directly at the creature. It bounced off a flailing claw and fell into the pit. Slumping back against the tree, Ancaeus wept.

Meanwhile, Evenor and Melanion had both raised their spears, ready to fling them at the crippled beast. However, the mantiger was spinning about and moving too erratically for them get an accurate shot, and they were desperate not to lose their only weapons in a futile attempt.

The swarming bees made it impossible for the mantiger to fly. Instead it dropped to the ground and bounded up the path away from the hunters, to some place of refuge.

"After it!" Atalanta cried. She'd already guessed where it would go.

CHAPTER TWENTY-EIGHT

ARROW'S FLIGHT

L ike any animal, the mantiger knew instinctively how to rid itself of a swarm of bees. As Atalanta had expected, it was heading along the path that led to the pool, the path where she'd set the snares.

A hideous roar told her that the mantiger had run straight into them. She only hoped the ropes would hold.

Rounding a bend, she was relieved to see the mantiger with the cords tangled around its hind legs, rearing up and ripping at the air with its claws. The bees were dispersing now in the open air, but there were still enough of them to distract and infuriate the great beast.

Skidding to a halt, Atalanta readied her bow. Melanion came rushing to join her with Evenor on his heels.

Before she could stop him, Melanion had charged straight ahead, yelling and thrusting the long spear at the mantiger's head. The beast seized the end of the spear in its jaws and, with one swipe of its paw, snapped the shaft in two.

Only now realizing his danger, Melanion tried to jump back, but the same paw smacked him across the head, sending him rolling across the ground.

"To me, to me!" Atalanta cried at the mantiger, trying to attract its attention so that Melanion would have time to crawl away.

For a second the beast hesitated, unsure, its golden eyes—now rimmed with swelling flesh from the stings—focused on Atalanta. It ignored Melanion, who scrambled back to Evenor's side, panting, exhausted, frightened, but unhurt.

Atalanta sensed her own danger, but kept calm, retreating step-by-step, staying out of the mantiger's way. At the same time she tried to aim her bow, but for some reason her arm was shaking too much to get off a careful shot.

Moving up to stand by her side, Evenor jabbed defensively with his spear, muttering, "By the gods, it's big. By the gods, it's huge."

Then one cord of the snare snapped.

And then a second, the sound of it as loud as the crack of a whip.

The mantiger suddenly lunged forward.

The unexpected movement caused Atalanta to shoot high and her arrow went past the beast's head, by no more than a whisker's breadth, and on into the trees. Quickly she nocked another arrow.

Evenor gasped out a prayer. "Hermes guide my arm." Then he hurled the spear with all his might. It ripped through the mantiger's right wing and grazed its back.

Rearing up, the mantiger trembled with anger. It bared its awful yellow teeth and beat the air with its wings, causing the blood to spray them both.

Evenor's spear fell to the ground, far out of reach.

"Artemis preserve us!" Evenor gasped, whipping out his knife. He reached down to grab Melanion's arm and haul him out of the way.

The mantiger crouched and then began its leap.

Atalanta pulled back so hard on the bowstring, the muscles in her arm felt ready to burst. Then she let the arrow fly and the string sang like the wind.

The arrow drove straight into the mantiger's eye, throwing it back on its hind legs. Its cry of pain was so loud, the trees shook in horror on each side of the path.

Dragging Melanion to his feet, Atalanta and Evenor backed away desperately. All they had to defend themselves now were their knives and one last arrow, feeble weapons compared to the monster's raking claws and long sharp teeth.

But the mantiger was no longer interested in them. Half blind, dizzy with pain, unable to fly because of its wounded wing, it turned away and ran off into the trees, howling. They could hear it trampling through the bushes as it made its escape, away from the world of men and traps, of arrows and spears and knives.

"Is it gone?" Melanion asked.

"Gone, but not dead," Atalanta answered.

"Then we have to go after it." Evenor was breathing hard. "Finish it off."

"Not *we*," Atalanta said. "Me. Evenor, you take care of Melanion and Ancaeus. Finishing off this beast is *my* job."

Evenor stared at her. "You are mad." He'd never looked at her that way before. "Girl, the mantiger may be wounded, but even wounded unto death, it's still more than you can deal with on your own."

Atalanta walked over to where Evenor's bloody spear lay on the ground. Picking it up, she wiped it off on the grass and hefted it in her hand. "This is far heavier than I'm used to, but it will have to do."

"Suppose the mantiger kills *you*," Melanion whispered, a pleading in his eyes. "How could I bear it."

She couldn't stand the way he looked at her, so vulnerable, so open. She turned away, staring up at the darkening sky.

"Melanion, you go and attend to your uncle," Evenor ordered. "I have to talk with Atalanta."

Melanion nodded. "Whatever you do, don't let her go alone. I count on you." He turned and stumbled back up the path.

"Atalanta," Evenor said softly. "Is there something you aren't telling me?"

She turned slowly and looked straight into his eyes. "Haven't you guessed yet, dear friend?" She reached down inside the neck of her tunic and pulled out the leather thong, holding the ring toward him so that he could see the engraving of the boar. "This ring, with the insignia of the royal house of Arcadia, was around my neck when I was found. The baby girl Ancaeus was talking about, the baby princess left on the hillside to die, with the bear tracks all around—that infant was me."

Evenor frowned. "You?"

"Look at my face, Evenor. Isn't it the queen's own?"

He shook his head wonderingly. "I hadn't noticed it before. But it's true—you look just like her. Iasus is your father?"

"My sire, but not my father. My *father* is dead," said Atalanta, "killed by that thing that the gods sent to punish the king."

Evenor looked out into the forest and rubbed his chin ruefully. "This business is darker than I thought. Who can fathom the ways of the gods?"

"I believe that the curse means that only someone of the royal bloodline can kill the beast," Atalanta said. "And that means me."

"You sound very sure of that," Evenor said. He rubbed the old scar on his arm as if that lent him strength.

"I *have* to be sure. A hunter can't afford to have doubts." She smiled. "That at least I learned from Orion." She stood on tiptoe and kissed him on the cheek. "Now go, my other father, go with Melanion, and don't breathe a word of what I've told you to anyone."

He nodded slowly. "We'll wait an hour, and then I'll come looking for you."

"If I haven't returned in an hour, get back to Tegea as fast as you can," Atalanta said, shaking her head. "For it will mean I am wrong in this, and the beast will be after the king next."

He cocked his head to one side and considered her for a moment. "Is that a doubt I hear creeping in?"

"That's called being careful," she said. "I learned *that* from my father."

Then she was gone, following the blood trail into the fading light.

CHAPTER TWENTY-NINE

THE CAVE

he mantiger left clear tracks dotted with blood. It was moving toward the mountains and, Atalanta guessed, heading back to its lair.

The worst kind of confrontation, she thought to herself. She would rather meet the beast—any beast—in the open. Once she and her father had cornered a mountain cat in its den. She'd been ready to charge right in, but her father had cautioned, "Leave it. We've time on our side. The beast will need water eventually. Nothing worse than your back to the wall in a beast's own lair."

Nothing worse than your back to the wall in a beast's own lair.

She could feel sweat breaking out on the nape of her neck. No, she didn't want to get into a cave with the creature. But if the mantiger denned, she'd have to go in after it. There was little time left. If she missed it in the dark, it would be after the others, her one chance gone.

The trail took a deep bend out of the forest and in the soft evening light, she saw she'd come to the foot of a mountain. About forty feet up was the black yawning gap of a cave.

She hesitated for a moment, thinking. It was the perfect cave for a flying creature, but the mantiger was on foot now. And hurt. Would it have struggled up? She checked the rugged slope for clues, but the stone held no prints.

If I go up and the mantiger isn't there, she thought, *I'll have wasted time. But if I don't go* . . . While she was thinking, she was also casting around for tracks at the mountain's foot.

You're afraid, she told herself, adding, *it's all right to be afraid. It's just not all right to be paralyzed by fear.*

She knew she wasn't a hero, but she had to do a hero's job. So she pushed the butt of the spear down through the back of her belt and began clambering up the rugged slope.

Finally, about ten feet up, she saw a streak of blood.

"Got you!" she whispered. It gave her added energy, and she almost ran the rest of the way up.

Soon she was hauling herself onto a narrow ledge that jutted out below the cave entrance, like the lower lip of a gigantic mouth. Scrambling to her feet as fast as possible, she pulled out the spear and stood ready to meet the mantiger's attack, knowing that if it leaped on her now, she could very well be flung into the void. If she fell forty feet—well, it might not kill her outright. There'd be just enough left alive to scream when the mantiger took out her throat.

When no attack came, she worked her way around so that her back was now to the rock face. If the beast went for her, at least she'd have one side covered.

Still the mantiger didn't appear.

Listening intently, she finally heard—over the sound of her own ragged breathing—an uneven, weak, labored rasp coming from the cave. Pushing the spear sideways, she edged around to the cave opening. Then she spun quickly to face the entrance and walked into the cave.

She could feel every muscle in her body. They ached with tension. She could scarcely breathe.

"This is for you, Father," she whispered. "And for Urso. And Orion. And Hierax. And . . ."

The mantiger was lying on its side near the entrance, its damaged wing uppermost, its wounded eye turned away. The other eye blinked weakly at Atalanta, but it had lost so much blood, it hadn't even the strength to growl.

As she looked at the dying creature, she felt both hot and cold. Something that tasted of iron and bile rose into her mouth. She swallowed it down.

"You've done enough harm for one lifetime," she muttered. "Now it's your turn to die."

Atalanta could see exactly where she needed to strike to pierce the mantiger's heart. Raising the long spear, she poised it over the creature's golden-orange chest.

The mantiger simply lay there, its ragged breath rattling in its throat.

Atalanta froze in midstrike. Through all her hurt and anger, she felt a sudden pity for it, this creature brought from its homeland, an unwitting instrument of the gods. She lowered the spear. Her father had taught her that a hunter hunted for food, respected the prey, didn't kill out of hatred, anger, or fear.

She took a deep, careful breath.

"Go in peace," she whispered to the winged beast.

As she watched, the mantiger's good eye closed and the tired heaving of its breast slowed to a stop.

How long she stood there, watching the creature draw its last breath, she didn't know, but the sudden scraping sound of claws on stone broke the spell.

She looked up and—a few feet farther into the cave—saw another limp form. It was a female mantiger, smaller than the male and without the majestic orange mane. It, too, was dead.

Even more amazing was the little animal cowering close by its side. The noise she'd heard had come from its clumsy attempts to nurse. It was a cub, its fur no more than a light covering of yellow fuzz, its wings small and immature. It looked weak and undernourished, and it shrank fearfully away from Atalanta.

"His mother died three days ago," said a woman's voice from the back of the cave. "She'd been weak ever since the birth." The speaker came into the fast-fading light. Tall and yellow haired, she was dressed in hunter's garb with a bow slung over her back. There was a golden nimbus about her, as if she walked in sunlight while all the rest of the world was dark.

The cub ran over to her, and she scooped him up in her arms. Stroking his fur absently, the huntress raised an amused eyebrow. "You know who I am?" she asked.

"Artemis of the hunt," Atalanta said, surprised and yet not surprised at all. "I recognize your voice."

The goddess nodded. "You've served me well, Atalanta," she said. "You hunted the beast as was your destiny and didn't shrink from the task. So I'll give you another chance to take your revenge. Kill this little one. I'll not stop you."

"I don't need revenge," said Atalanta, shaking her head. "Send the cub back to Egypt or Libya or wherever he comes from. He needs to be among his own kind."

"I'm not a Charon meant to ferry animals back and forth across the sea," the goddess said petulantly. "And it will be many long months before this little one's wings grow large enough for the task." She set the cub back down on the cave floor. "I doubt he'll survive that long."

Atalanta gazed at the mantiger cub and was suddenly

reminded of herself as an infant. Abandoned, she'd survived only thanks to the kindness of strangers, both animal and human. Setting the spear aside, she crouched down and held out her hands.

The little creature blinked curiously at her, then padded forward. She took him gently in her arms and lifted him up.

Stroking his downy fur, she said, "I'll see he gets milk and anything else he needs until he's strong enough to find his way home."

"Then if you don't want revenge, what reward can I grant you for your courage?" asked Artemis.

"Reward? I don't want any reward from you," said Atalanta.

"I always grant a gift to those who have served my cause well," Artemis said stiffly.

"As you did with Orion?"

The goddess looked away. "His pride was his own undoing."

"Yes, he was proud," Atalanta agreed, "and boastful, but he was also a great and brave hunter. You of all people should see he's remembered for that."

"Are you *telling* me what I should do?" the goddess asked. Her perfect upper lip curled in scorn. "One petitions a god, one doesn't make demands."

"Is one act of kindness beyond your power?" Atalanta asked.

"You've a sharp tongue, Atalanta. One day it will get

you into trouble," the goddess warned. "But I'll do as you ask this time, since I promised a reward. I'll set Orion among the stars so that his name will never be forgotten."

She raised a hand toward the heavens and as she did so, a dazzling light, like the first flush of dawn, consumed her. Then the light faded, and where the goddess had stood, there were now only shadows.

When Atalanta stepped outside the cave, the cub in her arms, she looked up into the night sky. There, where no stars had been before, were a group of twinkling lights. For a moment she could see him, the great warrior, with the lion skin on his shoulders, a spear and club in his hands, and around his waist a belt of three shining stars.

CHAPTER THIRTY

THE PALACE

hey returned to Tegea in triumph, even though two of their number were dead.

Struggling on the road to the city, Melanion and Evenor took turns helping Ancaeus, while alternately pulling a sledge on which they carried Hierax's body wrapped in the skins of the two mantigers. Atalanta walked alone, the cub in a sling on her back.

As they neared the city, the people they met hurried on ahead of them to deliver the news. A squad of chariots was sent to escort them into Tegea, and a grand procession formed behind them.

Women wearing white chitons and crowns of laurel sang songs of thanksgiving from the rooftops, tossing flowers down upon them.

The flowers made Atalanta sneeze.

King Iasus greeted the party in person at the gates of the city. He embraced his brother first, then clasped each of the hunters warmly by the hand.

When he saw the cub cradled in Atalanta's sling, he called for the guards. "Take that thing away and cut off its head."

"It's only a baby, a harmless baby," Atalanta said. "Artemis herself has put it under my protection." She glared at Iasus. "You don't believe in killing infants, do you?"

His face blanched, and he stammered a response. "It shall . . . shall be as you . . . wish, young huntress. I . . . I . . . I . . . honor Artemis. I will . . . *not* . . . go against her wishes." He called off the guards.

Atalanta nodded, but took the cub from her back and cradled it, like a baby, in her arms, letting it suck on her finger. Its milk teeth weren't strong enough to hurt. She rocked it for a bit, crooning a lullaby, and the cub whimpered a moment before falling back to sleep, snoring lightly.

Then Melanion told them all how—after Orion's death—it was Atalanta who'd devised the plan to defeat the mantiger, and that it was she who pursued it to its mountain lair.

"Without her, we would have had no chance," Ancaeus added. "No chance at all."

Melanion told the story again to the assembled court at a banquet in honor of the hunters. The story grew with the new telling.

If there's ever a third repetition, Atalanta thought, *I wouldn't be surprised if I flew up to the mantiger's cave on wings of flame.* But she smiled at Melanion because he told the story with such passion.

Ancaeus confirmed the story at the banquet. "But my nephew—my *courageous* nephew—has understated his own part in the hunt. Anything I've ever said against him, I now take back. I shall make him my heir as I have none."

The banqueters raised their cups to salute Melanion.

"To be the adopted son of a prince with the courage to be bait for such a beast would be an honor indeed," Melanion returned.

Once again the banqueters raised their cups, this time to salute the prince.

"And I," Iasus said, standing, "shall give Hierax's old place as royal huntsman to Evenor." The queen tugged at his robe, and he bent over to confer with her. Then he smiled broadly. "And we shall give the girl, Atalanta, any reward in our power to bestow."

Sitting on the king's left hand, Atalanta made a face. She didn't feel like being rewarded by him any more than she'd wanted a reward from Artemis. Standing, she told him in a shaking voice, "Just to be back and safe is reward enough, Your Majesty." Then she sat again.

He put his arm familiarly around her. "Nonsense. You *must* have a reward. Some gold. Some jewels at least. Marry my nephew!" He laughed and both Atalanta and Melanion blushed so furiously that the entire court rocked with laughter.

"I just want to go home," Atalanta said, brushing back a lock of hair that had come loose from one of the gold pins.

"And I," said Evenor, who was sitting next to Atalanta, "I'm a simple country man, Your Highness. From simple country people. My wife and children and I could never live here comfortably in the great city of Tegea."

Even so, Iasus insisted that Evenor be given a fortune in cattle and sheep. As for Atalanta, "You shall be treated as a princess, as though you're visiting royalty, and not . . ." He hesitated, unsure how she would take what he had to say. "Not just some wild girl out of the northern forests."

"But I *am* just a wild girl out of the northern forests," she said carefully, "even though your queen has graciously dressed me in fine clothing." She caught Evenor's eye and shook her head, warning him against saying a word more.

At the king's insistence, Atalanta had been installed in a huge chamber on the first floor of the palace. The room had colorful hangings on the walls and lush woven carpets. There was a bath sunk into the floor, towels, mirrors, perfume, even a bowl of milk in one corner for the cub.

After the feast but before the acrobats had begun their entertainment, Atalanta had gone back to the room, pleading a headache. She'd sent all of the servants away and closed the door behind them with a long sigh.

She sat for a long time on a little bench in front of a mirror of polished metal, and a stranger looked back at her accusingly. The stranger had glossy black hair set in elaborate curls, jewels around her neck and arms, tints of blue and green painted on her eyelids, and pink rouged into her cheeks. She was pretty—in an odd, brittle way.

Is this what a princess looks like? she wondered. If she told her history and produced the boar ring, she'd have to spend the rest of her life dressed this way, bejeweled and painted.

And then would I be Atalanta or somebody else?

She pulled off the jewels and threw them down on the bed. She took water from a bowl in her cupped hands and splashed it on her face to wash the makeup away. She pulled the pins and clasps out of her hair and ran her fingers roughly through it until all of the elaborate styling was undone. Braiding her hair, she slung it over her back. Then she began to strip off the beautiful, delicate gown.

When she looked back in the mirror, she recognized who she saw. Pan had said that Urso had to follow his own nature. Well, she knew that she had to do the same.

Going over to the window, she stared down on an olive grove at the back of the palace.

"Very splendid, isn't it?" Evenor said, coming in without knocking.

Atalanta turned. "It's only a room," she said, shrugging. "A place to rest and get out of the rain."

"We've a room for you back in Eteos," he said. "But it can't compare with this."

"When are you leaving?"

"In the morning. With the cattle and sheep the king has promised. Herma will have worked herself into a great passion by now, sure I've died. I miss her. And the children."

"You can't just leave me here by myself!"

"Be sensible, Atalanta. You're not by yourself," he said. "You *belong* here. You're the rightful princess of Arcadia. This is the home of your family."

"My family?" said Atalanta in a choked voice. "They left me on a mountainside to die."

He held up his hands. "Be fair, child. The queen knew nothing of that, and Iasus isn't the first man ever to act out of anger and disappointment. He has long since regretted his act."

"I haven't told them, you know. And I never will."

"Of course you will," said Evenor. "If not today, then one day. Truth is like good wine. You can't keep it bottled up forever. You have to share it." He leaned his head to one side. "I think the queen suspects anyway."

"That's why I must go—and quickly."

Putting his arms around her, he gave her a hug. "Whether you visit us as your friends or your subjects, you know that you'll always be welcome in our home."

"I know that, Evenor. Tell Herma and the children I will see them soon. I promise."

He left the room without looking back.

She locked the door behind him, turned, and threw herself onto the bed.

"I'll never be able to sleep," she whispered. But soon enough, sleep claimed her. She slept without dreams.

Dawn was just beginning to spread its rosy fingers over the land when she got up. Putting on her hunting clothes, she slung her bow and quiver over her shoulder.

"Maybe one day," she murmured to herself, fingering the boar's head ring. "Maybe one day I'll return to tell them the truth." She glanced out the window where a small wind was puzzling through the olive trees. "But not today."

The cub had stirred from its sleep and was rubbing its face with its paws. Bending down, she called to it softly and it scampered toward her. She caught it up under one arm.

"You don't want to stay here either," she said. "You'd rather be free under the sky. An eastern sky. Not an Arcadian sky where everyone still wants to kill you. But you're not old enough yet, not strong enough. So you'll have to stay with me a while longer."

She climbed out the window and onto a ledge. Tossing her bow and quiver and spear to the ground, she then lowered herself carefully until she was hanging on by one hand, the cub clutched in the other. Dropping the last few feet, she hurried into the cover of the olive trees.

"This is going to spoil the king's celebrations, you know," said a familiar voice. Melanion stepped out of the shadows into plain view. "He's planned a week of feasts, some even for the common people."

"What are you doing here?" Atalanta asked crossly.

"I've been watching your window all night, and . . ." He stopped, suddenly too embarrassed to go on. "You're leaving, aren't you?"

"Yes, and you have to promise you won't tell anyone," said Atalanta.

"Of course not, though they'll figure it out soon enough. I understand, though. I know what it's like to be cooped up in a stuffy palace when you can hear the outdoors calling to you. But we'll meet again."

"Did an oracle tell you that?"

Melanion grinned. "No, I just know it. Here." He placed his hand over his heart.

She put her hand over his. "I know it, too."

When she caught up with Evenor, she found him among the trees some miles north of the city. He had three shepherds with him, helping drive the cattle and sheep.

"Atalanta!" he said when he saw her, but there was no surprise in his voice, just pleasure.

"I'm not ready to be a princess," Atalanta said by way of explanation. "Not yet, anyway. I may not belong in the wild with the animals, but I don't belong here either."

"You're going to ruin their celebrations," said Evenor with a wry grin.

"So I've been told." She looked back down the road as if she could see Tegea. "They'll soon find someone else to gossip and sing about. As for me, I've had enough of kings and gods." She smiled and signaled the herders. "Let's go home."

WHAT IS TRUE ABOUT THIS STORY?

id the Heroic Age, the Age of Heroes, really exist?

Yes and no.

No—there was not a time when gods like Pan and Artemis actually took part in human affairs, nor was there ever a mantiger—a winged lion—preying upon the kingdom of Arcadia.

But, yes—there was once a rich and powerful civilization in ancient Greece, which we call Mycenaean, where each city was a separate state with its own king, but the people were united by a single language.

Arcadia was a district of ancient Greece, chiefly inhabited by shepherds and hunters. According to the poet Virgil, it was the home of pastoral simplicity and happiness, but actually it was a poor relative of the rest of the mainland, a mostly mountainous and infertile land, though grain was grown in some of the valleys. Surrounded on all sides by mountains, it has been called the Switzerland of Greece. Because of those mountains, when the rest of Greece was invaded in the Iron Age by the Dorians, Arcadia was left alone and the ancient speech of the Greeks survived there.

What also survived were anecdotes such as the one about Charmus, the runner, coming in seventh out of six runners, and a great deal of poetry. And—of course—stories. One of the most famous Arcadian stories is of the female hero Atalanta. She was known as a fantastic runner, and the story of her part in the Calydonian boar hunt was a standard in the Greek bardic recitations.

Did she ever meet Orion, the great hunter of myth, who was loved by Artemis and by the nymphs? Not that we know. But surely if these two hunters ever met, it could have been as prickly comrades. As for Orion's death, there are many stories—some that he died when Artemis shot him by mistake, some that a scorpion proved his death.

We have made up the mantiger, a combination of the dreaded manticore (a mythic beast that hankers after human flesh, born in the Indies with the body of a lion, the face of a man, a tail like a scorpion's) and the revolting Chimera (part goat, part serpent, part lion, with wings).

But we have not made up Astarte, who was one of the great Semitic goddesses and whose name appears in the Bible as Ashtoreth. She was the nature goddess of fertility and childbirth, as well as patroness of the hunt—so surely she and Artemis would have been rivals.

And what of Pan, the goat-footed god of flocks and shepherds and wild creatures? Arcadia was always the principal seat of his worship. He is described as wandering among the mountains and valleys there, either amusing himself with the chase or leading the dance of the nymphs. He loved music, invented the syrinx, or shepherd's pipes, and was dreaded by travelers whom he startled with sudden awe or terror, hence the word *panic*.

A woman like Atalanta—even a mythic hero—must have had a childhood and adolescence that foretold her future deeds. This is what we know from the old stories about her: She was the daughter of King Iasus (or Iasius) and Queen Clymene of Arcadia. Expecting a boy, her father was distraught when a girl was born, and so he had her exposed on Mount Parthenon where she was found and suckled by a she-bear. Some passing hunters discovered her and brought her home, training her up as one of their own. Her birth and youth have always been as a footnote to the later stories.

Those later stories are all about her heroic adulthood. Hearing about a monstrous boar sent by Artemis to devour humans in Calydon when the king there neglected to perform his yearly sacrifices to the goddess,

Atalanta took part in the hunt for the boar, despite some grumblings from the other hunters, all of whom were men. Only Meleager, the king's son, welcomed her. When Atalanta dealt the boar its mortal wound, Meleager gave her the spoils of the hunt. His uncles taunted her, and in a passion Meleager killed them and was, in turn, killed by his own mother. Atalanta then went back to her father's kingdom where she was finally accepted by him, for he had no other heir, and there she was expected to marry. She refused to do this unless she married a man who could beat her in a footrace. No one could until her handsome cousin Melanion (or Milanion or Hippomenes), having gotten Aphrodite's protection, won the race with a trick, using golden apples given to him by the goddess to tempt Atalanta off the track. They married and had a son who was a hero and was eventually killed in battle by one of Orion's grandchildren . . . but that's another story altogether.

We have taken the Atalanta of the legends and tales and projected her backward, using what archaeologists and historians have told us about the civilization she would have inhabited if she had been a real young woman.

Or a young hero.